KAFKA'S HOUSE

Gabriela Popa

Pixiphoria

ISBN: 0983864101

ISBN-13: 978-0-9838641-0-3

To my parents, Aurica and Neculai Popa

Contents

ACKNOWLEDGMENTS

The author would like to thank Mary Beth Wilczak, Susan Hume and Kathy Bratkowski for their friendship and their constructive criticism of this book.

Going to America

Ana and Crina Lecca are elderly twin sisters living on Milcov Street in Bacau, a quiet town nestled in the hills of Northeastern Romania. Like many other old folks in the city, Ana and Crina make ends meet by selling odd things, such as macramé, pickled cabbage heads and bors. I often buy bors, a sour soup stock made from fermented cereals and water, from them. I am always happy to help my parents by doing little chores, such as buying bread, bors, noodles or detergent for my mother or wine for my father. Whenever she needs bors, my mom gives me a raffia bag containing two empty milk bottles and says: "Silvia, why don't you go and buy some bors from Lecca sisters?"

As I said, Ana and Crina are old. They must be at least as old as my grandmothers, if not older. They live in a small house ten minutes away from us. Both sisters have countless brown spots on their skin, because they have a disease that my mother, who is a nurse, calls pityriasis. Taken together, the pityriasis and the smallness of the house terrify me. For some reason, I have always been afraid of people who live in small houses. Or maybe not really afraid - just uneasy about them. When, many years later, I visited Kafka's house in Prague, I was stunned to see how someone with such vast inner spaces can live in such a ridiculously small house.

Although I am always ready to help mom, bors in particular I don't enjoy buying. And that is because Lecca sisters are neighbors with the enemy. The enemy is Florin, a boy whose ears emerge at forty-five degrees away from the skull, like a donkey's. So every time we meet, I call him "donkey-head." He calls me "stork" because my legs, in his view, resemble those of a stork: skinny and way too long. The name calling clearly has some effect on Florin, because, to train his ears into obedience, he started wearing, now and then, a green elastic band over his head. His mother, Mrs. Lazar, knitted that green band for him. First, she knitted a white one. I remember when I first saw him wearing that white band: he had just come out of his yard, and was standing in front of his house, looking deliriously funny in his shorts and that band over his ears. He resembled one of those tiny soldiers coming back from war with funny clothes, sad eyes and his injured head wrapped in insufficient bandage. I was on my way home when he appeared in front of his house, looking up and down the street for children to play with. Two older girls, who were passing by his sidewalk, saw him and started laughing.

"Hi there, soldier!" one of them said to him. "Did you get hurt in the war?"

He became red in the face, looked at me, furiously and went back into his yard, slamming the gate.

A few days after that, he appeared with a green band on his head and refused to talk with me and didn't even bother to call me "stork" or such when I grinned at him. However, that didn't make his life any easier, because the green band, like the white one, was still something to tease him about. Simply put, before Florin, none of us had ever seen a boy wearing a headband. Headbands are for girls. It's that simple. Florin, we remark, giggling, is the first and only boy in the whole mighty Universe to wear a funny-looking green headband over his head.

On the other side of the Lecca house lives Mr. Gogu, an old man with perfect diction, who cultivates beautiful white roses and doesn't want to talk with anyone. People say he was a famous engineer in the '30s, before the communists came to power in Romania. My father told me that Mr. Gogu helped build the Vega Refinery of Ploiesti, whose oil filled Nazi planes and tanks during the Second World War. Often times on my way back from school, I stop by Mr. Gogu's fence. I like to watch how he pampers his roses, cleaning them of dried leaves and watering them during summers or wrapping them in hay and nylon sheets during the cold Romanian winters. To be honest, I am under the impression Mr. Gogu doesn't see or hear me, because he doesn't respond or even look at me when I stop and say, quite loudly and as politely as I can: "Hi, Mr. Gogu!" So once, about two years ago, I found myself singing a little song that sprung up in my mind as I was leaning on his fence:

Didn't wake the dream

Didn't pay the toll

Didn't die in peace

Didn't die at all!

He stopped his work and turned his head toward me.

" ...Didn't pay the toll... Didn't die in peace, Didn't die at all..." he repeated, slowly. "What grade are you," he asked, halting his work and coming to the fence.

"Second grade. I am eight."

"What's your name?"

"Silvia," I said. "Silvia Marcu."

"You are Aneta Marcu's niece... he said. "Now I see you resemble her..."

"Yes. She says so too. She says she gave me her gipsy eyes."

"And she did..." he said, looking long at me.

Then he continued:

"Where did you hear that song? Did communists teach you that song at school?"

What should I respond? What do communists have to do with my song anyway? Instead of responding immediately, I recalled how many times my mother told me to stop making up things.

"No, I made it up," I finally answered, embarrassed.

He didn't say anything. He turned around, cut a rose and gave it to me, patting me gently on my head, like my grandfather did. After that, he spoke with me every time I stopped by his fence and each time he told me that I was born during ill-fated times.

"Communism," he said, "is a cancer that sooner or later eats everyone's life up. When you grow up, Silvia," Mr. Gogu said, "never make any compromise. Never. Remember this, promise?"

"I promise," I said, holding tight the rose he gave me.

When I arrived home that day, my father and his younger brother, Tinu, were watching a soccer game and drinking wine.

"What does it mean to *compromise*?" I asked, entering the room with the rose in my hand.

"Sst! Shut up," said my father, "Ah, look at him! Look at this fool, he missed again," my father continued, pointing to a player on the screen. "What an idiot!" he sighed, emptying half of his glass.

"Well," Tinu said, taking a quick sip and turning toward me, "compromise means drinking a 10 lei wine when you actually would like to drink a 50 lei wine. Capisco?"

He then held his index in front of his mouth, meaning: we have more important things to do here, don't you understand?

"Capisco," I said. "Capisco."

Every time I go for bors, Crina and Ana ask me to come in.

"Come in, dear, don't stay there," they say.

I enter their house as if stepping on another planet. I never know what to say while I'm inside. During my first visits, while they were filling my bottles with bors (slowly, careful not to splash or waste a drop) I was staring with the innocence of my seven years at the spots covering their faces. There was something mesmerizing in the way a brown spot, covering part of the nose, hiked up on the cheek to slowly dissolve itself into a narrow thread on the temple. Each sister had her own pattern, otherwise they were almost identical. From the very beginning, buying bors was an extraordinary experience, mostly after I found out from my friend Duck what was *the real reason* for those skin stains. Duck had seen, in a book she found in her uncle's house, photographs of people looking just like Ana and Crina. Those people had been burned in an oven. Duck swore to me that in foreign countries they *do* burn people in ovens. After that, my terrors were even more terrible, and buying bors felt pretty much like going to war.

Holding the raffia bag with my two empty milk bottles and one leu and fifty bani in my hand, I knock at Lecca's door. As I look to the right I see some people in the enemy's yard, but I can not distinguish who they are because they are hidden by the grapevine screen. Crina Lecca opens the door.

"Good morning," I say. "Mom would like two liters of bors."

"Come in," says Crina. "Come in, dear, don't stay there."

She takes my bag and proceeds toward the table. There, without the slightest rush, she takes the bottles, one by one, out of the bag, and places them on the table. She folds the bag and puts it on a chair, to the right. By the table, also to her right, is the bors barrel, a large wooden container holding at least 50 liters, if not more. There is a pitcher, set on a glass plate on the table. Crina fills the pitcher carefully with a ladle, then places one of my bottles on yet another plate and starts pouring the bors in a steady stream. Right then, Ana enters the room:

"Ei, look who's here!" she says, gently ruffling my hair as she passes by.

I stand by the door and try as hard as I can not to think of or look at their spots. I keep biting my lips, trying to think of something to say. Suddenly it comes to me: I could find out if what Duck told me is true!

"Have you ever traveled to foreign countries?" I ask them as Ana wipes her hands with a towel and Crina pours bors with a constant thin thread, from the pitcher into the milk bottle.

"Ei, look at her," says Crina to her sister, "look at this blond mosquito, asking me if I have traveled to foreign countries."

She laughs.

"Yes, dear," says Ana, "a few times. I visited my friend Lucia who lives in Prague. I am going to visit her this summer again. She invited me there! She is a great poet, you know!"

Crina snorts, and mumbles in a little voice:

"...some great poet!" and keeps pouring bors.

"Sometime I would like to go to Prague too," I confess.

"Well, maybe sometimes in future, when you grow up a little bit, maybe you can come with me," Ana says.

"Oh, I'd love to see foreign countries," I respond.

"Ana, don't make promises you can't keep! You don't know if you are going for sure yourself!"

"I am going, Crina," Ana says. "Just get that in your head right now. I am going, and that's it. Period."

Crina snorts again, and keeps pouring bors.

Ana doesn't pay any attention to the sounds her sister makes.

"Prague is a very beautiful city, you know, they have churches with golden roofs, gold everywhere. All Prague is made of gold, Silvia. Those kings were very rich, those Czech kings. I received many postcards from her – oh, that's a beautiful country!"

A postcard! From a foreign country!

"May I see it, please?" I ask.

"What, you don't believe me? You don't believe me when I'm telling you that..."

"No, no, I do," I hurry to respond.

I feel blood rushing to my cheeks as I try to explain.

"But I have never seen a postcard from foreign countries," I confess.

"You wanted two liters, right?" Crina asks, holding the pitcher in mid air. She has filled one bottle and now cautiously approaches the second one. She places the bottle on the table, in front of her, on a flat plate. Then, with the ladle, very slowly, fills the pitcher about half. The ladle is then rinsed and hung on a hook over the bors barrel. It is always there, every time I come to buy bors: white, clean and shiny, its handle featuring a running band of yellow and red flowers.

"Yes, yes, two liters," I respond.

I like Ana so much better. She always smiles when she sees me, tells me stories about kings who cry with one eye and laugh with the other, and winks to me when her sister snubs her, as if to say "what does she know, this joke is just between you and me." Now, as Crina, slightly frowning, fills the second bottle with bors, Ana comes near me holding a notebook. It is a slim notebook, with black vinyl covers. On the cover the word *Dictando*

11

is embossed in shinny yellow letters. She pulls out a piece of paper – a letter - from the notebook. Wrapped in it, there is a postcard.

"Look at this, see? This is from my friend Lucia, from last year. This is Prague."

I take both the piece of paper and the postcard in my hand. The postcard is not new anymore, but still in good shape: just like money, dignified by human touch into leathery softness.

"See, here," Ana shows me, "here is Hrad Castle, see, among these woods..."

A sudden shriek from outside makes Crina's head raise violently and shake with spite:

"Ana, you forgot the gate! That pig is in hen's pen again! Can't wait to see him sausages and ham this Christmas! Get him out of there!"

"Go ahead and look at it," smiles Ana, and, placing the notebook on the mantel above the stove, rushes out the door, yelling in a high pitched voice, just as my grandmother does: "I-uu-i-uuuu-iuuuuuuuuuiiiiii!!!"

I keep looking at the postcard. So this is how foreign countries look: flat, with whitish blue skies, dark woods and majestic unreachable castles. I flip the card over: its other side is white. But the piece of paper, in which the postcard is wrapped in, is a letter, and because Ana handed it to me, I open it up and read it. On less than half a page, in minuscule handwriting, is a message signed by Lucia. As I read the letter, I try to invent Lucia from the way she graciously twists the s's, uniting them with perfectly curled a's and with straight, decisive t's. I read the text and here and there I stop for a second because I don't really understand it. I keep going, though, because the more I read, the more I get this mysterious feeling of traveling to exotic places:

Dear Ana,

In Prague everything would be beautiful if I wouldn't be so tired. Trying to see as much as possible, I am missing the essential, which, I believe, is the unseen soul of the city, its sobriety unmarked by the joyfulness so characteristic to us, Romanians... Today I saw on Zlatne Ulice one of the houses the great writer Kafka lived in...It is actually a room, room number 22, in a row of houses on the left of the Ulice, as you come down the street. Its colors are pink, muted green, whitish yellow, brown. Now it is made into a little bookstore, and it seems as unsuitable as a shop as it does as a house. As you enter, you go down a rather abrupt step and find yourself in a little hallway, which has to its left a tiny room, no larger than the space needed for a person to stand up. Everything - walls, ceiling - is painted white inside. The next (and last) is the main room, extremely short and narrow. In this room there is a counter where a woman sells paper souvenirs, mostly brightly colored papers, calendars, almanacs, and posters... It was very crowded inside. When I got out, the last two verses of a long-forgotten poem stayed with me for a long time:

I lived my life,

Pulling away from it, hence crushing it...

His fiancée visited him in this toy house? What books was he reading there and how was he sitting on the bed? There must have existed a house owner, a Mrs. Grubach, and a Miss Bürstner, tiny and delicate like the house itself. The townhouse two numbers further down has, toward the street, two fences that graciously curve in front of the door, enclosing a little garden. At the little garden - if it existed in his time - Kafka must've looked many times.

NB. The number of the house, "22" is painted in dark gray, with unequally drawn letters, as if sketched by a child who just learned to write...

Lucia

Ana, all sweaty and red, enters the room and goes to the water pail, fills a cup and drinks it into one long gulp. She sets the cup on the table nearby, but Crina, who's done with pouring the second bottle, notices it:

"Ana, why don't you put it back? How many times do I have to remind you to put things back *where they belong*? You are like a child!"

"Eh, right, who decides where they belong? You ?! Well, I don't agree it belongs by the pail and I don't want to put it there!"

Crina looks toward her sister as if ready to kill her.

"I'll teach you to put things where they belong," she mumbles.

"Isn't it beautiful?" Ana says, pointing toward the postcard.

"It is very beautiful, thank you!" I say, giving her back the letter and the postcard.

"You are welcome, Silvia."

She looks at them with love again then slips them in her apron's front pocket as if returning two beloved children to their womb.

Crina is done. She puts the two bottles in the raffia bag, gently arranging them so they are well balanced.

"Here you go."

There is noise again, outside. Crina looks at Ana:

"Did you close that gate with both hooks?"

"Sure did," says Ana.

"Well, if you would've closed it well, right now the pig wouldn't be chasing the black hen again," says Crina, looking on the little window above the bors table.

Ana raises her hands:

"That pig!"

She yells, getting out of the door.

"One leu for two bottles," says Crina.

I give her one *leu* and fifty *bani*: "Mom also wants some parsley."

"Very well," says Crina, "let's go outside in the garden and pick parsley." "Your mother is making *ciorba* today, ha?"

""Yes, she is making meatballs *ciorba* and chicken stew," I explain. "She said your bors is the best in Bacau," I flatter her, knowing Crina likes everyone to praise her bors.

"I take great care of it, Silvia dear, you know," says Crina. As she passes by the fireplace, she grabs the Dictando notebook from the mantle.

We are now in the backyard.   To our right (hidden by a row of bushes but very close, from what I hear) Ana is chasing the pig who is chasing the black hen. I hear her swearing: "Crazy animal! Come here! Come here, you vagabond!"

Crina starts picking parsley. She applies the same care, the same tediousness, careful to pick from here and there, and in less than ten seconds she has the bunch ready.   She wraps it in a sheet she pulls from the notebook.

"Here you go."

I thank her, I put the parsley in the bag and, still hearing Ana conversing with the pig - now the tone is rougher, the pig being called "total disaster," I leave the two sisters and their minuscule kingdom with black hens and crazy pigs.

When I close the Lecca's gate, I see the enemy in his yard, talking with three other boys. He is not wearing his green headband. All of them are laughing and looking toward me. I decide I am not going to pay attention to them, but Florin opens his gate, comes in front of me and tells me *no stork is allowed to pass in front of his house anymore.* As he keeps coming toward me, I take a step back. I prop up my bag against the fence and tell him to go away. It is only when he is very close to me, pressing me against the fence (those three boys watching and laughing) that, without any idea of what I am doing, I grasp his protruding ears and start shaking his head with fury. Instead of fighting, he freezes, then lets out a high pitch squeal, so loud that I let go, scared and almost deafened. In the next second he is running toward his house, crying for help. Slowly I step toward my bag, retrieve it and head home, stopping here and there for some flower or tree, but in reality, thinking only of the incredibly soft and hot things my hands just held and shook.

At home, my mother waits for me in the doorway, with her arms crossed and a resigned expression on her face. I open the gate and come closer to her. She keeps watching me without saying a word. This is not a good sign. Only when I arrive in front of her, my mother speaks. Her voice is low and her tone is serene:

"You are going to live for at least five hundred years, my dear child."

I know what she means. She means that I am so slow, that time will dilate around me so I can live forever, like some obtuse turtle. It also means that she's been waiting impatiently for me, that she was furious that I was so late. She is a nurse and she can not be late for work. She has to leave in one hour, and had planned other things besides cooking, things she won't have time for anymore.

"Five hundred years if not more," mom says again, pouring the bors in the pot.

"I beat Florin on my way back," I say, still breathing hard. "I pulled his ears till they were red like beets!"

"I don't know if this is something a girl should do," she says, her back toward me, working at the table. I seem to sense a chuckle in her tone, although it may be just my imagination.

"He called me a stork again! Said I could not pass in front of his house anymore!"

"Why is he calling you a stork?"

"Because I have skinny legs. And all the other boys laughed! Now they laughed at him, 'cause a girl smacked him!"

"Hmmm," my mother says, without looking at me.

As she unpacks the parsley, I notice the writing on the paper. It is the same handwriting as the one in the letter! I quickly grab it, place it on the nearby table, our dining table, and smooth it gently with my right palm. On top is written: Notes from Prague, 1967. Crina tore a written page from Lucia's notebook! Was this Crina's revenge because Ana never put things back? Or maybe she didn't even notice? I know I will find out about this next time I go for bors, but for now I have to rescue the text. Here and there the paper has creases and holes from the moisture. I rush to find my diary, in which I write all the significant happenings of my life.

"Silvia! What are you doing now? Go and take care of your sister, she is by herself outside in the yard!"

"I have to write something, mom," I respond from the next room.

"Don't you want to go out and play? Go and get some air, don't you see you are yellow like a lemon? Watch over Mirela!"

"I'll go later," I respond, my mind already captivated by the mysterious words on the paper.

Sitting at the table, I copy all I can understand from that page, word by word. I plan to secretly return the notebook page to Ana next time I go for bors. The page contains words I don't really know, things that, I figure, impressed the poet in Prague:

Literature museum

Manuscripts in leather and parchment:

Tiraguelli: Operum, Tom IV,V,VI,VII

Alexandri Tartagni: Consiliorum Libri 1,2,3

Haller: Epistolarum ab eruditis

Henrici Boceri: Disputationes

National Art Gallery

Long, rat paws, coming out from priests' stoles

Faces expressing a pain inflicted by flesh rather than spirit

Reptiles, having the same color as monks' garments, writhing under their long hems

Agnolo Gaddi (1369-1396)   A door crushing a black-greenish devil

Cornelis Saftleven (1607-1681) - Goats sitting at a table. The cat with a huge bird. Down, on the floor, among all these characters, a book

Carl Spitzweg (1808-1885) - A shadow of light behind the man, while his eyes search for an exit

Half an hour later, all done with my diary, I am out in the yard, playing with my friends and my three year-old sister, Mirela. Everyone jumps, runs, possessed by the game and a rebel energy that maintains all of us in continuous friction with the surrounding air. The yard is large, surrounded by a tall wooden fence. The house is owned by my aunt Aneta. Every room has a door toward the yard; some of them also have doors toward the rooms on left or right. The great majority of tenants start their tenure in aunt Aneta's house by renting one room, and living in that room all together (parents, children, sometimes a grandparent or a nanny) until their finances allow them to expand to the next level of luxury, two rooms. Our family occupies two rooms, one of them being declared the kitchen because it contains, set on a little table, the gas burner, a rudimentary stove where my mom cooks the most delicious stews, steaks, sour soups that use the bors I buy almost daily, and my favorites, *sarmale*, ground meat with rice wrapped in grape leaves that are oh so divine. In the kitchen, on a massive wood bed inherited from my grandmother, my sister and I sleep. There is also a large table where we eat and I do my homework. The other room, containing again a bed, table, cupboard and a radio, is mom and dad's room.

We are all hot - it's a beautiful May afternoon - and play one game after another, tirelessly. Marin, a skinny boy with big blue eyes, says:

"Thugs an' turkeys!"

And suddenly the whole crowd shifts its strategy and the new game is instantly accepted by everyone.

As I am running and hiding behind trees, so I don't get touched by turkeys, I stop, because, as it will happen many times in my life, a thought has exploded with such force in my mind that I cannot stop or ignore it. Like many other times, to understand it better I look into some imaginary dot, somewhere at two thirds distance between me and the closest object. Slowly, as I start seeing it, I say:

"When I grow up, I'll go to America riding a cow."

Everyone around me stops - because it is not clear if the sentence is part of the game, and waits for me to start running again, being one of the major thugs at the moment. But I don't move, and Duck, my friend, touches me with her palm on my shoulder, as she runs in circles around me. When someone touches you, if you are a thug you become a turkey, i.e. a cop, and vice versa. I am impermeable to these transformations, stunned by this understanding that I'll travel to America riding a cow. The game is now over, and some of my friends become interested in my trip.

"What is America?" my sister Mirela asks.

"It's a county," I explain.

"Why do you want to go with a cow to America," Duck says, "why aren't you riding a horse, like everybody else?"

I consider the question and after a second I explain that it's much better with a cow, because America is far away - long trip - and if you have a cow you at least drink milk, while from a horse you have what?

"True," says Duck, meditatively.

Everyone now stops running and, sitting on the grass or leaning against trees, discusses foreign countries. Mirela, my three-year old sister, understands that her sister leaves for some exciting place and comes close to me:

"Silvia, will you take me with you to America?"

I reflect a bit:

"I can't, Mirela, even then you are going to be little, and besides, this is an adventure, I can't promise you anything..."

"Please," says Mirela, who understands she is being left behind, "take me with you!"

"No," I say, "I can't."

Mirela's eyes are full of tears and her voice is shaky. She starts crying, first slowly, then sobbing, loud enough for the few adults that are at home to hear her. Mom comes rushing out of the kitchen.

"Why do you cry, Mirela honey, what happened?"

"She doesn't want to take me with her, she won't..."

"She? Who? Who?"

"Silvia, she ...won't take me."

"Take you where?"

Everyone explains to mom that I, who will be leaving with a cow for America, don't want to take Mirela with me.

Mom laughs and caresses Mirela's face.

"Don't cry, Mirela sweetie, Silvia is not going anywhere. She was just joking. Where is she going to travel - don't you see that I don't have money to go anywhere, how is she going to leave for America now? Don't cry these lovely tears, she's only joking!"

But Mirela cannot be calmed down. Her hiccups become spasms and her face is all blue. Mom doesn't have time for this, she is already late for work. She looks at me and says:

"Silvia dear, tell your sister you'll take her with you."

To my own and everyone else's surprise, I utter distinctly:

"No, I am not taking anyone else with my cow to America!"

Mirela, all blue in the face, lets out a long wail, and having exhausted her lachrymal resources, falls to the ground as if shot. Mom, who's late for work and whose stew is burning on the stove, doesn't care that what she's negotiating is pure fantasy. She identifies a quick solution that never fails: she grasps my hair with her right hand and pulls a few times:

"Take your sister with you to America, you stubborn goat!"

Taken by surprise, I burst into tears, which automatically calm Mirela, with whom mom leaves, holding hands and talking softly. I stand there, among my friends, crying and swearing in my mind that now -

more than ever - I must go to America and then further still, to a charmed country no other humans - Mirela included! - know of and never will, because if they even think of going there with me, Boom!! they become orioles, and no one around them will understand their obscure chirps in ten thousand years.

What do you want to be when you grow up?

Although I expected Florin's mom, Mrs. Lazar, would come by to complain to my mother, that didn't happen. Mrs. Lazar, who is a hairdresser, didn't say a word to my mother, even when my mother went, a few weeks later, to have her hair done. I am thinking about this as I am preparing to go to school. I am also thinking that Duck - when told about my encounter with the enemy - said I should've kept pulling till his ears came off. I imagine the enemy earless, floating around like a pot without handles. I snicker as I put my notebooks and books in my schoolbag.

"Stop giggling and drink your tea. And don't forget your sandwich," my mother says.

I take the sandwich and put it in the sandwich box. This is a metal box painted in bright colors on the outside: a spotted cow grazing silently in front of a barn in whose window a chicken head raises a red comb, stiff like a flag's pole. I looked so many times at this box, at its every corner, its every edge, that I almost know it by heart. If I close my eyes I see it under my eyelids in full color. On its bottom is written, on a small oval shiny label, *Made in China*, a foreign country about which I do not know too much except that its people are called Chinese, that there are many of them and they all speak a weird language. This impression of the Chinese language came to me from hearing Mrs. Popescu, our teacher, ask some boys in our class, "Am I speaking Chinese to you or what??" after she told them many times (and of course to no avail) to sit still and stop talking among themselves. I also have a book with Chinese tales - a gift from my father for my birthday last year - which I have read many times, over and over. Chinese tales are quite different from the Romanian ones. Each of these Chinese tales has a grain of bitter wisdom, like the one about the magic salt stone dumped by a greedy peasant down into the sea. Which is why, the story says, the seas are salty, I explain to Duck as we walk to school in the morning.

"Why did the peasant dump it into the water?"

"It was a magic stone," I respond. "It could spin by itself and so salt poured out of it. And the peasant was so poor that he didn't have any salt, so he stole the magic salt-grinding stone. But of course he was too greedy and ground way too much salt, and the salt filled his house, his yard, and everything else. And he was in danger of being suffocated by all that salt, so he started pushing away the stone. And pushed it and pushed it till he reached the sea shore, where the spinning stone fell into the sea. And it kept grinding salt at the bottom of the sea, and still does....and because of all that salt, the seas are all salty now..."

"I don't care too much about this story," Duck says. "For one thing, salt is cheap. Why would someone bother to steal a stone made of salt. And second, a stone made of salt cannot be magical. If it were made of gold, I agree. Or diamonds. But salt," says Duck as we take the corner on Morii Street, "salt is not a big deal *at all*."

"Hold on, girls, hold on, now!" A man raises his hand toward us, then yells to his coworkers:

"Go on, team, push it! Go ahead!"

About ten workers have blocked Morii Street and are now digging right in the middle of it. Except for the guy who stopped us, who has blond hair and looks cleaner, they are all dirty. Dust and oil cover their clothes, hands and faces. All of them handle strange machines, which raise clouds of steam and dust and make sharp noises. The Morii street is narrow, paved with cubic granite stones. The workers have removed a section of stones a few meters long and are now digging in about three places. Meanwhile, other people have stopped as well.

"Why are you digging," yells an old man with a beard and dark glasses, trying to be heard over the noise. "Has some pipe burst open?"

"No, we just found gold," the blond worker responds seriously, coming closer to us.

I look at Duck. Duck looks at me. GOLD!!! On Morii Street!!

But the worker continues:

"Of course a water pipe broke! What else do you think?"

"And can't you respond in a civilized way? Isn't it enough you stopped us, now we have to endure your saltless jokes?" says a woman carrying two bags full of potatoes and onions. Those bags must be pretty heavy, by the way she looks. She has large dark circles around her eyes and her bluish, thin lips sag into an almost comical expression.

"Ei, don't be so upset, madam," says the blond worker, looking at her bags, "or your soup will come out too sour..."

As he says that, he winks toward one of his coworkers.

"Who do you call madam," says the woman, now really furious. "I didn't rub my shoulders with you. You should learn to be respectful to people around you; I could be your mother!"

"All right, now, that's enough," the blond man says, and, raising his hand, yells at his workers: "Stooooop! Now! Halt! Halt!"

The workers stop their machines, rendering the clouds of dust immobile for a few seconds. They rub their sweating foreheads with the back of their hands. Some of them spit. Some of them cough. They wait in various positions, among the clouds of dust that connect their bodies with fantastic, smoggy appendages.

"All right, you can pass now!" the worker says to all of us. "Go on, go home now and make your soup! Take it easy now!"

The old man and the lady with bags pass us, and we hear them talking:

"Can you believe, Mrs. Velea, how badly behaved these workers are? When I was young and no one had ever heard of communists, a worker knew the length of his nose! Do your work and don't take airs like you are the Master of the Universe! Now they can stop you, they can block your street, they can do whatever they want...You know what they'll do? They'll dig and leave the hole right there in the middle of the street for weeks now!"

They pass us, and their voices become weaker and weaker.

"Did you learn by heart the poem for today?" Duck asks.

"Yep. I did."

"I can't recall a line," she says. "I rehearsed and rehearsed but now I can't recall a line. Wanna rehearse together?"

She is trembling with fear.

"Sure. Let's rehearse."

Duck's parents are very strange. I don't like them at all. In particular her father is a dull, unpleasant man who never smiles. Maybe he has a reason for that: Duck's brother, Adrian, is a handicapped child. He was born with one extra chamber in his heart and because of that his face is blue, his lips are big and purple and he cannot talk, although he is three years old. But the real reason I hate Duck's parents is that they beat her. If she comes home with a mark below 7, they beat her with a belt. A leather belt. Duck showed me many times the bruises, all over her back and buttocks. Many times, Mrs. Popescu asks Duck to sit straight on her chair (not leaning toward one side) but I know Duck has a hard time doing that because her bottom really hurts. When she believes she doesn't know something for school, she almost goes nuts. I tell her to calm down, because how can you concentrate and remember something if you are freaking out?

"Let's rehearse," she says again. So she starts:

"My Party? Oh, my Party is the sea

That carries us to our brightest dreams,

The mountain with the whitest peaks of glee…?"

She stops.

"The mountains with what….? ..Aaa, what is this, peaks of glee? Mountains have peaks of stone, not glee!"

"Come on," I say, "don't cheat! Go on!"

"OK," says Duck, "you're right! Aaa, ...*glee*...I forgot! This is the line I can't remember!"

"Do you want me to tell you?"

"No, hold on, hold on a second...If you tell me I'll forget again...*White peaks of glee..?*"

She stops for a second.

"What is there...No, don't tell me..."

She starts walking again, mumbling softly:

"Peaks of glee..well, I can't remember," she says, "but I don't want you to tell me..."

She puffs air through her lips, disappointed.

"I am going to remember...oh well, I can only remember the last line of the second stanza: '*Its strength? my strength! Its future? my own future!!…*'"

"I can tell you the first word, if you want," I say.

"No, don't, I'll keep thinking till we get in the class, I rehearsed it all day yesterday..."

We enter the school yard. Everywhere you look you see children. Some are shouting, some are running, some are silently moving toward the entrance doors. In a few minutes, we are in our classroom. While Duck mumbles softly: *whitest peaks of glee...* over and over, I keep thinking what if they actually *did find* gold on Morii Street but they're pretending it's a broken pipe, so people don't steal it!! When we reach our desk, Duck takes her schoolbag off quickly, gets the reading book out and opens it, exactly when Mrs. Popescu, our teacher, enters the class and says:

"Good morning, children."

Duck puts the book aside, stands up like everyone else and says: "Good morning, Mrs. Popescu!" then whispers to me, terrified: "She's looking at me! She's going to quiz me!!"

Mrs. Popescu looks around the entire class – there are about 25 of us, boys and girls. Her eyes stop for a fraction of a second on everyone's face.

She opens the roll, the dreaded roll where our names and marks are, and takes the attendance. Then she looks at us again for a few seconds, and says:

"Claudia Neamtu, do you want to come in front of the class and recite the poem for today?"

Duck gives me the look of a person condemned to death and slowly stands up, then drags herself to the front of the class.

"Come on, come on," says Mrs. Popescu. "I don't see a lot of enthusiasm. But before that," continues Mrs. Popescu, "today, from 9 to 10 - this is next hour, children - we'll have inspection. Mr. Inspector will come with two of his students and will ask you questions. Mr. Inspector is a very nice man who teaches university students - he is very kind indeed. It is a great honor that he chose our class for inspection. When he asks you a question, stand up, say your name and answer politely the best way you can. All right, now, Claudia, let's hear the poem, are you ready?"

Duck, all red and shaky, bursts into tears.

"What is it," asks Mrs. Popescu, "why do you cry?"

Duck starts crying even harder, so hard, that her shirt shakes as she tries to speak. Tears fall on her face in waves, and her eyes are red from how much she rubbed them with the back of her hands.

"I don't..remember...a line..." she says, between hiccups, "I can...not remember ... I rehearsed yesterday all day long..."

Mrs. Popescu's tone is mild and kind.

"But this is not a reason for crying...tell us what you remember, come on.."

Duck cannot stop crying at once, but after a few sobs, she manages to calm to a certain extent. Still breathing unsteadily, as if she had run for miles, she starts reciting, and her tone is so unusual that I don't know if to laugh or cry myself as well, as I sit at my desk and watch her. She says, in a whining tone:

"My Party, oh, my Party is the sea

That carries us to our brightest dreams..."

She stops, and looks toward me. I am in the second row, behind little Marin. As I see Duck approaching the critical moment, I place myself behind Marin as snugly as I can, and mimic toward Duck, who's looking at me, transfixed:

"Defending!!!?"

I try to be as expressive as I move, soundlessly, my lips. I stretch my lips into the best "D" I can possibly master, then I whisper again:

"Defending our borders!!"

"The mountain with the whitest peaks of glee"...continues Duck, and then keeps repeating "peaks of glee." I repeat again: "Defending!!!"

I am so captivated by my efforts that when I feel a hand on my left shoulder, I don't react. I look up and see Mrs. Popescu, standing tall and looking at me. I see her red lips, her exquisite eyebrows, her freshly done hairdo.

"Why don't you say it a bit louder, so everyone can hear you?"

I feel the blood rushing to my face. I have no idea how she's got near me, how is it that I didn't see her leaving her desk.

"Come on," Mrs. Popescu says, "louder!"

So I do. I repeat the line that Duck couldn't remember on her way to school. It's no wonder she couldn't remember it, because it didn't rhyme with the rest anyway.

"Defending our borders with its glory!"

"All right," says Mrs. Popescu, "Claudia, you can take your seat now. Silvia, would you like to come in front of the class and tell us what this poem means?"

As I exchange places with Duck, our eyes meet. She looks really scared. She is taking her seat. I go, apprehensive, not knowing what to expect, toward the blackboard. I look at it: the black hole, able to destroy your life forever. All you have to do for that to happen is write there, on the blackboard, under Mrs. Popescu's eyes, that 7 X 8 is 42, like I did last week. Among the many things that make my life terrible, the multiplication table is the most recent. I cannot help looking for long seconds to the dark blackboard, and even higher, toward the space above it, where, aligned in perfect order and neatly framed, are the color pictures of the Central Committee of The Communist Party, starting with Tovarasul Nicolae Ceausescu. They all look at me with their well-rounded, well fed, satisfied faces.

"What does this poem tell us, Silvia?" Mrs. Popescu asks.

The class is silent. I look over it and I see the enemy, Florin, with a large happy grin over his face, extending from one ear to another. Little Marin looks at me with his beautiful, kind blue eyes and a candid smile on his face. In the very last row, I see Nedelcu, who's repeating the class for the third time, probing one of his nostrils with his index finger.

"In this poem," I say, repeating what I read in the manual, "the poet depicts the Communist Party. The Party is as strong as the mountains and as infinite as the sea."

"Gooood," says Mrs. Popescu.

"Moreover," I continue, "the poet tells us that the Party will carry our people into future, like a ship carries travelers on the infinite waters of their dreams."

"Aaa, very gooood. Very good, Silvia. You really understood this poem. These are very good answers, children, and if Mr. Inspector asks you, this is how you should respond. However, Silvia, you tried to cheat today. I am going to give you a mark that will remind you not to cheat in the future. I'll give you 10 for your response and 1 for your cheating, so your mark today is 5.50, rounded to 6. You may take your seat now. As for you, Claudia, I will forgive you today, but I'll quiz you next time on this poem and the one we'll learn today. Understood?"

"Yes," says Duck, standing up.

I slowly go to my seat. A six is bad, very bad. I never had a six in my life. I had eight at math. But six, never. I don't know what my mother and father will say or do. I think extermination. I am so saddened by how things have turned out that everything around me seems to have lost its substance and color and became a fake, sustained by some artificial energy I do not understand or approve of. The inspection hour seems unreal. Mr. Inspector came indeed, but instead of asking us about the Communist Party, he asked us if any of us went to see the elephant exhibit at the Museum of Natural Sciences. And now he wants to know what we want to be when we grow up. This last question makes everyone antsy.

"Driver." "Professor." "Singer." Nedelcu wants to be tractorist, that is a tractor driver. He wants to have his own farm and raise sheep, like his grandfathers and father.

"This is good, children...our country needs tractor drivers as well... we need workers, construction workers, builders, we need to harvest our rich soil and build the socialist society of tomorrow... It is a great honor to be a worker and work with your hands, because the working class is the cornerstone of our society, children. They make up the most important layer of our socialist society, children."

After Nedelcu, Mr. Inspector stops by little Marin's desk.

"And you? What do you want to be when you grow up?"

Marin blushes, stands up, leaves a second of silence, strategically, and in a powerful voice, emits:

"Ambassador!"

A wave of laughter shakes the classroom. The Inspector smiles:

"Very well. This is a very beautiful profession. I wish you success, I hope you will become ambassador and represent our country all over the world!"

Marin sits down, proud. He turns toward Duck and myself. As always, he has the kindest smile on his face. Now, he also has a special light in those beautiful blue eyes.

We are now going home, Duck and me, slowly carrying our schoolbags and not talking too much. Although my schoolbag is not heavy, that six in my mark book feels like lead. It has rained heavily, it seems, and there are pools of rainwater here and there in the schoolyard, around which we step carefully as we walk toward the gate. Now and then a drop falls on our heads or faces. It only takes a few moments though, and the sun is coming out of the clouds again. I like the smell of the rain. The smell of the grass, still oozing with water. The asphalt, cooled down. Every blade of grass, all the leaves on the bushes and trees shine with droplets of water, so heavy that the leaves themselves bend slightly as the drops progress toward the soil.

Finally Duck asks:

"Wanna stop at my house first, before you go home?"

"No, I have to go straight home," I say, "I have to get Mirela from aunt Aneta. Mirela," I explain to Duck, "is staying now with my aunt from noon, when she gets home from kindergarten, until two in the afternoon, when I arrive home. I have to give her something to eat," I continue. "Then, she has to take a nap. But why don't you come to my house after five, I say, we can do our homework together."

"OK," says Duck.

I am thinking that now, with this six, it's going to be impossible to convince mother and father to let me go to the seaside camp in August. I want so much to go to that camp! But then, what could I have done differently? Duck is my best friend. The best I ever had. We spend most of our time together and know a lot about each other. And most of all, I like her because although she has terrible parents and a handicapped brother, she is always happy and frisky like a cat and has all kinds of astonishing ideas. She makes me laugh every day - the way she mimics professors, the stories she tells about her relatives, the voices she makes when she sees me upset.

As we come out of the school yard, we stop and look. A new kiosk has emerged since this morning in front of the school, right there on the curb. Lots of pupils stop by and look at it. Everyone wants to get close to the little window where the head of a woman with blond, short curls becomes visible if you stand on your toes.

"How much is a *gogoasa*?" a pupil asks.

"Fifty *bani*," responds the woman.

Duck and I get closer and look inside the kiosk. There, on a metal table, the woman has a boiling pot with oil and a pot with liquid dough. She takes a ladle of dough and slowly pours it in the boiling oil. The dough quickly assumes a contorted shape and in a few seconds has become a wrinkled, golden *gogoasa*. The woman picks it up with a huge needle, places it on a large metal tray and pours powder sugar on top of it. Then, she hands it to the older boy who ordered it. I look at Duck. Duck looks at me. It must be so tasty! The boy bites, and the sound – crunchy! the satisfaction in the boy's eyes, all tell me that I must ask mom for 50 *bani* tomorrow.

We are about to leave when Duck, who managed to get quite close to the window of the kiosk, stands on her toes to see better inside, then thinning her voice and speaking like a stuttering four years old, asks on a high pitched tone:

"Do-do-do you have *go-go-gosi* with c-c-coconut c-c-c-cream and English butter?"

The woman doesn't even look at her, preoccupied as she is to pick every golden *gogoasa* that floats, light like a foamy island, in the oil, but the pupils around us, mostly boys, hear Duck and burst into laughter. The blond woman turns toward Duck, who has a serious face and asks again:

"B-b-but *go-go-gosi* with fried mushrooms, mustard and eggplant puree d-d-do you have?"

The seller considers for a second then responds, in an irritated tone:

"We don't have any *gogosi* with coconut cream or mushrooms, girl! Why don't you go home," she says, to all of us. "If you don't buy anything, get out of here, go home! What do you think this is, a zoo? Get out of here, now!"

Laughing, we depart, Duck with a winning smile on her face. After a few more steps, she points to the house on the corner. We come close and I see what she means: from the gutters, a thin thread of water in the form of elongated drops falls down onto the asphalt.

"Look at this," she says.

She takes her backpack off and hands it to me. Then, she takes her pullover off so now she is in her blue uniform. She comes close toward the thin thread of drops that fall from the gutter, and holds the back of the shirt collar away from her neck skin. She positions herself so that the drops fall in a thin thread right on her spine. She shudders with joy:

"Aaaa! This feels so good! This is so good!"

She shakes like a cat, then after a few seconds pulls away from underneath the gutters.

"Aren't you wet? What if you catch a cold?"

"Naaa! It feels too good! Try it!"

I feel her shoulders and her back. There are a few wet spots on her shirt, but they don't even come close to the joy that I see in her eyes.

"Wanna try it? It's gooood!"

"No, I don't," I respond. "I don't like my back wet at all."

"You don't know what you are missing....you should try it sometime," Duck says, putting back her pullover and taking her backpack back. "It's great! It invigorates you. It's better, you know, than..."

"Than *gogosi* with mushrooms?"

And we both laugh as we turn the corner onto Morii street. Even from more than 100 meters we can see the hole that the workers have dug this morning. As we get close, we see that it is longer now - twice as long as it was this morning - and deep. I try to get a glimpse inside. I can distinguish some mud, water and stones at its bottom. It is primitively encircled by some mounds of cubic stone and some piles of wood on one side. People pass by and stop to comment: "Look how they left it, how senseless these workers can be. If you fall inside, you are dead! Little girls," a man says to us, "don't stay so close to it! It is dangerous!"

"We just wanted to see what's inside," I explain with as much dignity as I can. "We want to see if it's deep," I pretend, although what I am trying to do is see if anything glitters on its bottom, in which case it may indeed contain gold.

"It is deep all right," says the man. "Better stay away!"

We don't respond, and continue our walk home. As we turn onto our street, Milcov Street, out of nowhere the enemy and two boys appear in front of us. The enemy grins:

"The stork got a six today, right?" and laughs.

"Go away!"

I am ready to get to his head again. But he's careful now and doesn't come close to me. Instead, he asks his friends:

"And what are we going to cook today for lunch? Eh? *Rata pe barza?*"

And saying that, with a sudden move, he pushes Duck into me, with such force that Duck loses her balance and falls over me, and I fall on the stone pavement on my left side, hitting the ground pretty hard with my hip and scratching my left arm and hand, as I try to stop the fall. We twist, inefficiently, back and forth, because our heavy school backpacks prevent us from quickly rising from ground. The boys celebrate with undisguised joy:

"Ha, ha! Here's your lunch! Featuring the best dish for today! *Rata pe barza!*"

Rata pe varza is a dish. It means duck (*rata*) on cabbage (*varza*). *Varza* is one consonant away from *barza*, which means stork, the nickname the enemy invented for me. They leave laughing, as we manage to get up, with tears in our eyes. We walk home limping, both of us. Ten minutes later, I arrive at aunt Aneta's, who lives across from our house, to get my sister. Aunt Aneta sees immediately that I am limping.

"What happened to you?"

"Florin pushed me and I fell in the middle of the street..."

"Why did he push you?"

I shrug.

"He just pushed me."

"That boy is crazy, no wonder those ears come out of that head like in horses! I am going to tear those ears out next time I see him! Does it hurt badly? What if you broke your leg? When is your mother coming home?"

"At four," I say. "No, it doesn't hurt too much..."

"Well, make sure you tell her, you may have to go to the hospital, if it hurts bad later on," she says. "Your mother is a nurse, she will know."

My sister Mirela enters the room and comes close to me.

"Here you go," says Aneta, handing me Mirela's coat. "She's been very good. We just had lunch."

"Thank you, aunt Aneta," I say. "Mirela, let's go home."

Mirela takes my hand, and we walk home, Mirela jumping, me limping. It's good we live so close to aunt Aneta: all we have to do is cross the street and we are home. Mirela wants to carry her green and yellow kindergarten bag that mom just bought for her. She puts it proudly on her shoulder.

"Silvia, do you know what I did today at kindergarten?"

"No, what," I say, looking left and right as we prepare to cross the street.

"Our teacher asked me what I want to be when I grow up..."

"And? What do you want to be when you grow up?"

She caresses her kindergarten bag affectionately.

"Mailperson," she answers.

As I unlock the door, Mirela asks:

"Silvia, can I sleep with my kindergarten bag?"

"Sure you can. Just make sure it's empty, OK?" She jumps in the bed, joyfully, and I cover her with the blanket, and tuck the blanket around her beloved kindergarten bag as well. Then I go in parent's room, take the round mirror from the hook, get my uniform off and look at my left hip: it is red and swollen like a tomato, and hurts terribly when I touch it. My left arm also hurts badly. I return to the kitchen and look in the pots on the stove. Mom cooked chicken with sour cream. She always leaves food for the two of us on the stove in a little pan, so I can easily warm it up. I like chicken with sour cream a lot, but now I don't feel hungry. I put on my pajamas and sneak in the bed near Mirela, who sleeps smiling with her beloved bag in her arms. Looking intensely in the ceiling, I mull over my miserable day and my many wounds, among which the six at reading hurts the most.

The drunk and the tailor

Sometimes things are strange and they turn in my favor when I least expect it. Although I expected my parents wouldn't care about my encounter with the enemy, that was not the case at all: my father became red in the face when I told him how the two of us, Duck and I, were bullied by Florin Lazar. That evening, without even eating, he immediately went out to Florin's house and spoke with his parents. When he returned he looked at me and said, in his most serious tone:

"Let me know if he's creating any more troubles for you from now on."

His face was serious too, something I am not used to because most of the time he is jesting or otherwise making fun of me or the people around him. But this time I heard him and mom talking in low voices in their room, and although I couldn't distinguish everything, I could make sense of certain fragments. I heard him saying: "Is it possible, Mrs. Lazar, I say to her. Is it possible? My child could have died right there, in the middle of the street...hit her head on the pavement... this is not play...please take the necessary measures..."

My father likes to use big words. He always behaves as if he's speaking with distinguished unseen people who follow him everywhere he goes. Always behaving as if there is a secondary audience to whom he is continually presenting. Instead of saying: "take care of your child," he says: "take the necessary measures." He tells me that my tale books "intoxicate" my mind. When he opens his mouth, my mom teases him, he talks as if delivering some speech in the Parliament. My aunt Aneta says he is the most gifted man the Marcu family ever had. And if he hadn't liked paharul (that is, "the glass," meaning plum brandy) too much, he could have become Minister of Finance instead of being an accountant in a factory. But my mother says father could not have been a Minister of Finance in a thousand years because his father, my grandfather Ion, was *chiabur* which means that he had land and was rich and the first thing communists did when they came to power, after taking away people's land by force, was to make sure that the children of *chiaburi* never got anywhere in life. No *chiabur* son could have been Minister of Finances in a million years.

So I guess all my father can do under these circumstances is to imagine that he is the Minister of Finances and speak to everyone as if they are members of some important official body, as he did with Mrs. Lazar.

The doctor who saw me gave me two days of home rest, so my leg recovers. I am now, after these two days, pretty bored with lying in bed, so when my mother and father discuss which of them will go to buy bread and bors, I offer. I wanted anyway to see Ana and tell her about the torn page.

"I'll go," I say to them. "I can walk now."

"Not this time," says father. "You can't carry anything. Your leg is still frail."

"No, no, I feel good, really. I have to go to school tomorrow anyway."

"Let her go," mother says. "It's not a bad idea for her to move a little. Tomorrow she has to walk for half an hour to school. And I only need a liter of bors. It's not that heavy."

With my empty milk bottle in the raffia bag and fifty *bani* in my hand, I walk slowly toward Ana and Crina's house. My leg still hurts but much less. In my pocket, neatly folded, is the precious page with notes from Prague. I knock at the sisters' door. Ana responds, and opening the door for me says:

"Come in, dear, come in, don't stay there!"

She takes my bottle and places it on the table. I follow her and she notices my slight limp:

"What happened to your leg?"

I open my heart. I tell her how Florin pushed me and Duck, and how we fell on the pavement.

It is not often I see Ana frowning like that.

"Silvia dear," she says. "Florin is a very bad boy. You should stay away from him. I see his mother beating him almost every day. Two days ago he drove her so crazy that she took the shoe from her foot and

57

smacked him. I don't know what's going to become of him. You should not come even close to him and never, never play with him. You have to promise me that."

"I know, but if I try to stay away he comes and looks for a fight...My aunt Aneta said he's worse than the devil..."

"Aaaa!" says Ana. "You should never, never pronounce that word! It's a great sin!"

"But it's true," I say, "he..."

"Well, even if he is, you should never say the word...don't you know," she says filling the bottle with bors, "don't you know the story of the drunk and the tailor?"

"No, I don't, will you tell it to me... ?"

"Of course, because I want you to remember my advice."

She puts the bag on the table and sits on one of the chairs by the table. She invites me to sit on the other chair.

"There were, once upon a time, a drunk and a tailor," Ana says. "The drunk was a man good at heart, but he liked plum brandy a bit too much and did nothing else all day long but drink. He didn't work hard either - just barely enough to pay for his booze. He could never hold a steady job and his family - his wife and kids - left him. He was spending most of his time in pubs with his lowly friends.

...Now, you see," Ana continues, looking in my eyes, "in the same village there lived a tailor. The tailor was a lonely, quiet man who didn't have any friends. All day long he worked, and worked, and worked. He lived by himself in a dark house and sewed until his fingers went numb. He never smiled. And one day," Ana says, "what do you think happened? They both died, the drunk and the tailor, and their souls reached the gates of heaven where God sat, in his Holy Kindness. God looked at the drunk and looked at the tailor. And again looked at the drunk and looked at the tailor. What should he do with these two souls? So after a few moments of deliberation, He allowed the drunk to enter heaven and sent the hardworking tailor to the hell. When the tailor heard God's will, he started crying: 'But God', he said, 'why do you send me to hell? All my life I worked from dawn to midnight and earned every cent with the sweat of my brow. Why do you send me to hell and this drunk, this louse who never did anything good in his life, goes to heaven?

'Well', said God, in His Holiness, 'I'm glad you asked this because it's time you understand, tailor. This man, although he drank all his life, every time he drank he thought about me and said *Blessed be God's name! Honored be God's name here on Earth and in Heaven!* Thousand of times in his life, before touching the glass of plum brandy with his lips, he said those words. You, on the other hand, you stood in your lonely house and sewed all day long and every time you pricked yourself with the needle you spoke the devil's name, over and over. This is why, God said, he goes to heaven, and you go where the one whose name you spoke thousand of times, lives'.

...And this is the story," Ana says, standing up and arranging the bottle in the bag. "Remember to say God's name and never, never to curse. It is a great sin to curse. And if you ever hear people cursing," she says, giving me back my bag with my bors bottle, "pretend you didn't hear it. God is all powerful and hears and sees everything..."

"This is a very beautiful story," I respond.

"Well, next time, when we are alone again, I'll tell you another story," she says, smiling and patting me on the top of my head.

I retrieve my 50 *bani* from my left pocket and also the page from the Dictando notebook. I first give Ana the money, then, unfolding the page, I show it to her:

"Last time I came, the parsley was wrapped in it..."

She takes it and placing it on her left palm, she smoothes it with her other hand, tenderly.

"My sister cannot stand Lucia...If she could, she would stop her from writing me letters anymore... And she would do anything to stop me from going there this summer, but I will go... Lucia is my only friend."

She folds the page in four, and puts it in her apron's pocket.

"Take care now, walk slowly. Take care of your leg and don't even come close to Florin. If you see him coming toward you, go away. He's a really bad child, I told you. Two months ago, he killed our cat. I'm pretty sure it was him. Who else could've done it, Mr. Gogu? I told his mother, but what can the poor woman do? This boy will become a criminal one day. When I asked him if he killed the cat, do you know what he did? He grinned. He didn't say no. I wish he wasn't my neighbor, you know..."

As I walk back home I think there is nothing I like more in this whole world than tales. I could read tales from morning deep into the night, if my parents would let me. With all my chores - school, Mirela, buying stuff - I can barely get half an hour of reading every day. And even so, even after I'm done with my stuff, when I'm deep in the story and the prince enters the forbidden room, or the princess is being brought back to life, my father pushes his bold head through the half-opened door and says:

"Silvia, I forgot to tell you to buy some pasta...would you like to go and buy some?"

"But, dad, I only have two more pages!!! I can't go now!!"

Who am I kidding: by now I should know it's not worth fighting.

"Leave that book," my father says. "You are intoxicating your mind with garbage! You're reading lies, all day long! Go out and breathe some air!"

So I go out and breathe air while buying cacao, pasta, bread and such. And while doing that, I walk back and forth (carrying bread or bors bottles or whatever it is I have to carry) like characters in Romanian tales do: without the slightest of worries, nonchalantly discovering what's around, and without the slightest trace of a purpose. The more I think about this, the more I see it's true: take for example the story of the man who leaves his house disgusted by how stupid his wife, children and neighbors are. He walks for years in search of smart people but instead he keeps meeting dumb and dumber people, over and over. He keeps looking, the story says, until he wears out seven pairs of steel shoes. He learns to talk with birds and wolves. He fights fantastic creatures with infinite powers and reaches lands that are so beautiful that they enchant his dreams for the rest of his life. And, while doing that, he learns that there are, out there, people thousand of times more stupid than his wife and children, and so he finally returns home, old and wise, to die happily in the middle of his own brood.

In a way, my father is right: I live more in an imaginary world than in the city of Bacau. I am on a constant lookout for miracles. To me, it seems totally possible that a tree may anytime open up a mouth at the bottom of some branch and start talking to me. Finding gold in the hole on Morii Street seems as possible to me as holding my breath at will. Anything can happen, and I am on a constant lookout for the slightest sign that I am suddenly the main character of some extraordinary tale. But right now things are tough: trees refuse to talk to me and the only creature with hideous powers and mischievous ways is the enemy. My hip still hurts after our encounter three days ago, but I am not limping anymore. I had, however, to go to the hospital with my father and have X-rays done. No bone was broken, but my hip is still swollen, so I am excused from physical education for one month. When children run around during breaks in the schoolyard, I sit aside, on a bench. But God watches and sees everything: one day after the enemy pushed Duck and me, he got the mumps. His donkey head is now connected to his trunk through a neck swollen like a funnel, and his spectacular ears now sit on two huge swellings the size of onions. He stays at home and stares out of the window for hours. And if he gets out of the house (which he's not supposed to do) and stands in front of his house, swollen and frowny, everyone (even his friends) crosses the street and walks on the opposite sidewalk, at a safe distance from him. He's missing classes, among them our math class, where we learn the multiplication tables.

...Math. I don't understand how someone can like math. Although I know how to add or subtract, it all seems irrelevant and nondescript. The multiplication table itself is nothing but a torture instrument, and I cannot comprehend who brought the world such a miserable creation, whose only purpose seems to be the torment of children. I spend endless afternoons at home repeating: 5 X 8 = 40, 4 X 9 = 36, 4 X 3 = 12. My father, who is an accountant, cannot admit he has a child who's slow with numbers. He knows by heart all 246 phone numbers of his business contacts for the factory he works in. For him, numbers are like water. Indisputable. Indispensable.

We are outside in the yard, on the bench by the old pear tree. It is warm and sunny. I have to learn the multiplication table with 7 and 8. My homework was to fill in results for multiplication operations, one column for 7, one column for 8. So I did, and now father inspects my homework. Other neighbors are outside as well. Behind our back, I hear aunt Aneta, our landlord, talking with a few of my friends - her disobedient little tenants. She is upset that children go and play close to her garden, a narrow patch by the back fence where she grows cucumbers. She just noticed that someone walked among the vines, she can see little footprints there...

"If I see one more child playing around my cucumbers, I'll beat you all *de va zvint!*" This is an old Romanian expression that means *till I dry you out*. It applies mostly to rugs, which were dried by being beaten.

"*De va zvint*, hear me? I told you thousands of times: if you step on cucumbers, they become bitter! I didn't plant and water them for you to embitter them. Hear me!" says aunt Aneta one more time, closing the gate as she is leaving our yard.

Father opens my slim math notebook. It only has 12 pages left, out of 48: the others were furiously torn by him when he found mistakes in my homework. This is the third time in the last two hours he quizzes me. I hope three is a charm, because the previous two times I didn't get too many answers right. Father skims through my exercises and says:

"Seven times six."

I have to go step by step: I know that seven by five is 35, so I add one more 6. 35 plus 6 is 41.

"Forty one," I say.

Father doesn't say a word anymore. Instead, he closes the notebook, and Paaaaf! smacks it right on the top of my head. I shake as if someone has hit me with icy water.

"How much did you say? How much is six times seven?"

I cannot utter a word, because I feel a knot right in my throat. I try to swallow it but tears fill my eyes. I absolutely cannot think now: my mind is blank like a sea of milk. Seven times six doesn't amount to anything.

"Seven times six," my father says.

I first inhale, and then exhale with a hiccup, on the cusp of which I start crying. I cry on my behalf. Self-pity envelops me like a fog, and pity has soft and tender arms, and she is good and soft like a mother, and she understands.

"Rehearse them one more time," says father. "Get these numbers in that empty head of yours."

Toward the back of the garden, my friends play with a ball. Father goes inside, and as he enters our kitchen I hear him telling my mother:

"Say, seven times six is forty-one now, according to your daughter!"

I sit on the bench, with the notebook on my lap. I look at the first column, and read, in my mind:

7X5=35

7X6=42

7X7=49

7X8=56

The difference between them is seven, not six. I should have added 7 to 35. But that, in itself, carries no meaning, no true content. Instead, the more I look at the rows of numbers, the more I see them as part of a story. This does not help my situation at all, since father will be back to quiz me again. But I can not stop seeing it: a large trumpet, like a musical toboggan with white and flexible ends, extends now from 35 to 42, and through it the seven dwarves slide, one by one! Voila! This is how you make 42 out of 35! Then the dwarves, who by their nature are fidgety creatures, travel to the next operation, and hop! What do you think? 42 becomes 49! Numbers become alive under my eyes and jump around, among golden trumpets that now accompany the sounds made by my friends who play with the ball. And I sit on the bench, staring off into space, and I follow the dwarves around, hopping up and down from one ladder of the multiplication table to another, up, down, up, down, and I see their red and sweaty faces, and I smile at their red clownish costumes, and little do I care that I still have to learn the multiplication table with eight as well, 'cause right now they all came alive, all of them, and they talk with me, and laugh, and sing, and we are all having the time of our lives.

Marin

It is not the noise, but the tone with which one of my friends playing toward the back of the yard says "dead" that wakes me up from my reverie. Something is happening because although I cannot hear clearly what's being said, I see them staying still for too long. I hear fragments of sound: "Let's go! Let's go!"

At the same moment Duck enters the courtyard; she came to do her homework with me, as discussed. I put the notebook and math book down on the bank; I wave hi to Duck and rush toward my friends. Duck joins me.

"Little Marin died," Liviu says, seeing me approaching. "Fell in the hole. He had blood all over his face, he had clotted blood in his eyes," says Liviu. "He had clotted blood all over his eyes, and hair," Liviu keeps repeating, looking at Duck and me.

"What? Little Marin??"

"He died!" Liviu says again. "He fell in the hole, the hole workers dug on Morii Street. He fell and broke his head. And I was passing by and I saw many people. And a man jumped in the hole and held him up and other men pulled little Marin over, but he was dead. Then the ambulance came. And they took him, but he did not move and everyone said he was dead. Then some people said they would go to tell his parents and I went with them to show them where his mother lives, but she was not at home, and her neighbors said she was at work."

Liviu is so excited that his freckles - a pale yellow - are reddish-brown now. He keeps saying "clotted blood" and Cristi, another boy, says "Let's go" but no one moves. When aunt Aneta comes again to water her cucumbers, everyone rushes to tell her about Marin, and everyone speaks fast, fighting for her attention, and you can see aunt Aneta is overwhelmed by what she hears, and when Liviu tells her that Marin had clotted blood in his eyes she puts her hand in front of her mouth.

"*Doamne fereste*, God forbid," she says, "how did he fall?"

"I don't know," Liviu says, "but he had clotted blood in his eyes and his hair. And he didn't move at all."

"Those poor parents, may God have them in his mercy!" she says, crossing herself.

In the next second, Duck and I run toward our house. I start yelling before even opening the door.

"Mom! Moooom!"

"What is it," mother says coming from the next room. She holds a stack of white pillowcases she wants to iron before leaving for the night shift.

"Mom, Marin died!"

"What? *Ce spui*? What are you saying there?"

I tell her.

She doesn't seem to understand my words. She frowns, as if I've done something terribly bad myself.

"Marin, our classmate, died, Mrs. Marcu," Duck says to her, in a soft voice. "He fell in the hole they dug on Morii Street. Liviu saw him dead."

My mother doesn't say a word. I expected that she would say something like "Don't you say," or "Oh, my God." Instead, she froze with that frown on her face. So did my father, who entered the room when Duck was explaining.

"How is it possible," father says, "for those workers to leave a hole like that, wide open, in the middle of the street, for days now? How can someone be so irresponsible?"

"What do you expect from them," my mother says.

"This is why," father says, turning toward Duck and myself, "this is why your parents always tell you girls to be careful. Always watch where you walk. See what tragedies can happen if you're not careful?"

Half an hour later, Duck and I are sitting at the table by the window and do our math homework.

"Eight times four," says Duck.

"Thirty two," I respond.

She has to OK it, and then we verify one more time by checking it in the book. Only after that, and slightly sighing, we write it down in our notebook and end it with a well-rounded, glorious full stop:

8 X 4 = 32.

Then it's my turn:

"Eight times seven."

"Aaaa...fifty six."

I think about it. Somehow eight times seven is the most difficult of all. This one, and seven by nine.

"Fifty-six," I confirm, after I check the book. And we enter it:

7 X 8=56.

Duck looks around. Then she stretches her neck toward me.

"You know they keep growing, right?"

"What?"

"His nails. And hair."

"?"

"When you are dead," she mutters.

I still don't understand.

"What are you talking about? What nails?"

"After you die," Duck says, "your nails and hair keep growing. So little Marin's nails and hair will keep growing even when he's deep down, buried in his coffin."

"It cannot be," I respond. "If you're dead, you're dead!"

"Yes it can. The hair and nails are not alive. You cut your hair and you don't feel a thing. It's independent of the rest of your body, don't you see? And you know," she continues, "what happens after that?"

"No."

"I know."

"What?"

"*Strigoii* appear, don't you see? When your nails and hair grow very long, you suddenly wake up from your coffin and start running after people with your huge nails. You become a *strigoi*." She projects her hands toward me like a witch.

"These are lies," I say, "and you know it!"

"No, these are not lies, Silvia. These are true things."

"How do you know?"

"My grandma saw two of them with her own eyes! She saw two *strigoi* in the back of her house when she was a child."

"It's not true. Little Marin cannot become a *strigoi*. Only bad people can become *strigoi*. He was a very good child. He was going to become an ambassador."

Duck thinks about it.

"Maybe you are right. But even so, even if he's not going to become a *strigoi*, his hair and nails will still keep growing."

I imagine little Marin dead, surrounded by waves of hair all around his dead body, until all space in the coffin is taken up by the sinuous curls of dead hair, until, in a blessed end, everything starts rotting, decomposing into nondescript pieces of weightless material.

I don't respond.

"You don't believe me, do you?"

I shrug my shoulders.

"Well. When I was at my grandma's last summer," Duck says, in a low voice, and pauses. "When I was there, she asked me to go in the chicken pen and get a chicken for her."

"So what?"

"So I did. She wanted to make chicken soup for me. So, she took the chicken, held his head and neck on a big tree stump in the back of her yard and with an ax, boom! she chopped its head off! What, you don't believe this either?"

"This, I do," I say. "My uncle Vasile does the same when we visit them and they prepare chicken for us. They have lots of chickens and hens. And ducks. And geese."

"Well," Duck says, "do you know what happened after she cut its head off?"

"What?"

"The body - without the head - started jumping around and blood was gushing out of the neck like from a fountain! It was splashing in all directions! And the body jumped around ten times before it finally fell on one side and didn't move anymore!"

"It jumped ten times?"

"Ten times, just like that! *Tzop, tzop, tzop,* ten times! All around us. And all this time blood was splashing all over the grass. Then suddenly, it fell on one side, and my grandmother picked it up and took it in the kitchen and she scalded it with boiling water and then we plucked all the feathers. So, you see, although it was dead it still jumped around like a live chicken."

Now we are both silent. For one thing, I don't know about nails and hair, but chickens moving after their heads were cut off I have seen myself as well. But they were barely bending a leg or a wing, not jumping up and down like Duck says. And I never thought they were alive while doing that - but who knows?

Next day at school there are no classes. We go in, and find our teacher Mrs. Popescu and Mr. Manea, our school director, standing by the window and talking in low voices. Mrs. Popescu asks us to sit down, and then tells us that a tragic accident happened and one of our classmates, Marin Ionescu, has lost his life. She talks in a low, sad voice. Tears come to her eyes and she pauses for a second, and then looks at Mr. Manea.

"This is a terrible, terrible tragedy, children," the school director says. "And this terrible tragedy happened because Marin played near a construction site, something a child should never do. As homage to your colleague, we organized a trip for you to see him, all of you, on Saturday, before," Mr. Manea says slowly, "before Marin Ionescu is buried. A bus will drive you there on Saturday morning and Mrs. Popescu will be with you. You should learn from this tragic accident," he continues, "and never play on the street or near a construction site."

At home, my mother asks me if I really want to go.

"You don't have to go, if you don't want to," she says. "This is not a place where a child should be. I don't know what's with that school director and that Mrs. Popescu."

"But I want to go," I respond. "All my colleagues will be there. And it's the last time I can see little Marin."

When I tell my aunt Aneta that they are getting us into a bus to see Marin before he's buried, she crosses herself.

"That Manea must've lost his mind. What did he tell you about the accident?" she asks.

"He says that it was Marin's fault because he played near a construction site."

"I'll tell you whose fault it is," Aneta says. "Those workers who left the hole in the middle of the public road, they are the guilty ones, not an innocent child! They should be held responsible and punished! That Mrs. Popescu of yours would do better to load all those

78

criminals on a bus and drive them directly to jail. All of them. So they don't get a chance to kill other children."

Two days later - as they said on Thursday - here we are on an old bus, driving to Marin's grandmother's house in the village of Galbeni. In the bus everyone is noisy, yells, even fights (Nedelcu and some other boys) but as we arrive, everyone is eerily silent. The bus stops in front of Marin's grandmother's house, a small, poor looking building surrounded by a dilapidated fence. The yard is full of people of all ages dressed in black. They stand, talk. Cry. Most of them are old women, with wrinkled faces and curved noses. One of the rooms in the front of the house - a little one, without windows - is the mortuary room. Mrs. Popescu asks us to form rows of three and enter that room.

Inside, there are flowers all around, and the room has a table in the middle, covered with a white tablecloth, on which sits the coffin. Marin has dahlias all around him, around his head, around his little body. On the table, among flowers, there are many crosses, made of wood and metal. In a corner of the room - up, where the edges of the walls meet - there are many candles, all burning a heavy oil smelling of basil and myrrh. It feels like a one-room church. The walls are covered with wood icons from which the elongated, severe faces of saints stare at you.

They had put four chairs by the corners of the table and there we sit, each of us, for half an hour, when our time comes. Before or after we are done with our half an hour of wake, we are told by Mrs. Popescu to go outside and sit on some other chairs, in front of the house. I sit on one of those chairs, outside, and look over the garden. I look intensely at the beanpoles, at some green bushes planted toward the back of the house. I let my eyes rest on the corn stalks. In the front of the house, a large number of dahlia flowers are raising majestic, almost haughty red heads. I look for what feels like hours over that garden, until I feel oddly tired. A curious sensation comes over me, a calming certitude that I am as old as all those wrinkled women in the yard. At 11 o'clock Mrs. Popescu comes out and tells me it is my turn to go in for half an hour. As I enter the house, Duck's shift gets out. I look at Duck and she looks at me and there is no expression on her face. She doesn't make the slightest sign to me, she doesn't smile and she doesn't frown. She just walks out with empty eyes.

Maybe because of Duck's stories about *strigoi*, the only image that stayed with me over the years was that of little Marin's hair. Marin's hair was brown with blond streaks. I knew all the nuances quite well because I sat in the desk behind him in the classroom. Some bangs were yellow, so you could say he was blond, and you weren't mistaken at all. And just above his forehead, he had a little vortex that twisted a bunch of blond hair into a minuscule hayrick. I always liked to look at that little bunch of unyielding blond hair, which had a different shape every day because he was always tousled, always running his hands through it, combing it into a heap of brown and blond hairs. Now, dead, they – someone - had combed his hair dutifully, from the top of his head toward his forehead. The hair obeyed. It was now laying in unequal waves, and covered his head without reason or discipline with an incoherent haircut. The tips of his bangs ended just above his eyebrows into a wavering, trembling line.

As I sit on the chair, looking at the yellow walls and the yellow face of the dead, I hear a noise outside.

"The priest! The priest!" a little boy announces, entering the room.

There are many people talking in low voices and making a noise like rippling water getting closer and closer. Then the door opens wide and people, young and old and all dressed in black, enter the room. They keep their faces down and cross themselves. All four of us pupils stand up. The groups of people split and in the middle I can see the priest, chanting words I do not understand in a grave, beautiful voice. The priest is a man with a black beard, dressed in a long black cassock. He slowly steps toward the coffin carrying a silver candle attached to a long silver chain that he swings back and forth as he comes closer and closer. A strong aromatic smell - myrrh and heavy oil - comes off his silver candle, and quickly fills the little room. The priest's voice is so deep and grave, and resonates so powerfully among the poor walls that tears come to my eyes.

"Dumnezeuuu sa-l ierte pe roobul sau Mariiin...." sings the priest, coming step by step closer to the table. "May God forgive his slave Mariiin..."

The priest continues to sing a low, sad and melodious song, imploring forgiveness for the child who departed for the never-ending journey.

"His soul," the priest chants, "white as the whitest snow..."

Everyone cries. Almost everyone who could enter the tiny room did: Marin's mother, his grandmother, old women from the village. All stand, holding their faces down. Tears run from red, old eyes. Marin's mother cries so much that she doesn't have a voice anymore. She only says "Marinica, wake up, Marinica!," a name that carries with it a desperate caress. She says "Marinica!" with a hoarse voice, a no-voice whisper. As the priest sings, from time to time she whispers "Marinica, wake-up, Marinica!" and covers her face with her hands.

Pain doesn't come naturally to a child: it has, perhaps, to be learned. The priest's song, the smell of burned myrrh, little Marin's unnaturally peaceful face: all fill the room with an emotion so intense, so abrupt that I have to breath deeply and lean on the wall to remain present. I try as much as possible to define my space, to protect myself from this flood of emotion that comes to me from all senses. I keep looking at Marin's forehead, at the wavy hairline until everything else, the priest, his chant, people around me, all become a second reality, possible but strangely remote.

I don't know how much time passed - minutes or hours - until Mrs. Popescu enters the room and tells us that we have to leave. We all get into the bus. My eyes sting. But worse than that, I am very hungry. I could faint with hunger. I quickly find a seat toward the middle of the bus and lean against the window. Hunger sends painful throbs through my stomach. It inhabits my head. The other side of death, its twin sister, called survival, is now a river flowing through the bottom of a hole filled with stale pipe water, and I am not sure now if this is where our bus is taking us to or from. I close my eyes as the bus's engine cranks and then starts. We move. We are alive. A few minutes later I barely hear the nondescript voices of my colleagues around me. Hunger inhabits me and digs long channels, left and right, through my body, and it is painful and it is good. I fall asleep in that warm sound around me: the sound a hive would make if I were tiny and tender, tiny like a flee, tiny like a butterfly, like the tiniest bee...

A few months pass after the terrible, terrible tragedy, as Mr. Manea names it, and nothing happens to the hole on Morii Street. "Walk on the sidewalk, not in the middle of the road. Don't play near a construction site," our parents tell us. And the hole remains, as the man with beard and dark glasses predicted, open and menacing for more than three months. And then one day, the workers come and fill it with sand and dirt. After one more month they repair the pavement. By then, they are digging another hole on another street, because some other pipe had burst open.

At school, the seat in front of me remains empty.

The Sea...

Sunday afternoons are the worst. I'm done with my homework for tomorrow. I'm sick of the multiplication table with seven and eight. I can't think of any game to play with my sister. Even worse, I don't feel like reading a book right now. My mind is revolving around what Mrs. Popescu, our teacher, asked us last Friday: who wants to go to summer camp in August 25th? I want to go with all my heart, but I am afraid to just go and ask my parents. So, not knowing what else to do with myself, I stand in front of the window and stare. Somewhere, at the periphery of my visual field, raindrops tirelessly orchestrate myriads of dances. There are many stories in those dances: some drops fly together and collide with the glass in a high drama act, then run sinuously in rivulets only to converge into a fat drop, slow and deformed, that disappears half a centimeter away. Other drops never unite with others: they are loners, persisting on millimeters-long adventures only to disappear when lured away by some blind spot where I cannot study them anymore. The drops come and go, over and over, as the rain keeps falling.

"What are you staring at?"

From her tone I realize that my mother has been watching me for some time. I don't respond. She comes closer, stands behind me and looks outside. I see on her face that there is nothing outside to be stared at.

"You were watching something, what was it?"

"Nothing," I say.

"What do you mean nothing; you looked like you were seeing something."

Aha! Maybe now would be a good moment. Maybe I should just try.

"I was thinking" I say.

"Oh yes? And what were you thinking so deeply about? The immortality of the soul?"

"I was thinking," I say in my most serious tone, "that Mrs. Popescu asked us last Friday if we want to go to the summer camp, at the Black Sea. Mom, could I go to the camp, mom? Mrs. Popescu said that all of us should go...could I go, please?"

"Please don't start this again, Silvia dear. I thought we settled this discussion last year. Don't you see we barely have money to buy food? Don't you see we can barely pay the rent?"

My father enters the room with a glass of wine in his hand. He bought a bottle of red wine because in fifteen minutes the soccer game starts. His favorite local team plays, and Tinu, his brother and my uncle, will come by any minute, to watch the game with him. I am afraid to ask my father about the summer camp. He always says no to anything I ask him.

"Where does she want to go now?" he asks, as if just vaguely interested in the topic.

"To a summer camp," I respond. "To the seaside, to the Black Sea..."

"*Ei poftim*! Well, now!" my father says. "Do you want to drown in the sea?"

"But other children go there, dad, it's not only me...Mrs. Stroe already told Maria she can go..."

"Since when do we match up with Maria's mother?" my mother says. "Don't you see Mrs. Stroe spins money around like a witch?"

"Why do you want to go into the unknown," my father says. "What is this fanatical wish that possesses you to always go somewhere? Always to go? What's wrong with staying at home and playing with your sister? Why do you want to go into the unknown, to lose yourself into this crazy world...?"

"But we are not going into the unknown, dad, we are going to Constanta! By train! And many other professors are coming with us...And mom, Mrs. Popescu said we don't have to pay now, we can pay later on...it's four months from now, on August 25th...."

"Drop it," my mother says. "Don't you see we simply don't have the money? If we had the money, do you think I wouldn't let you go?"

But my father doesn't say anything about money. He only talks about *the dangers*.

"What, do you want to go and drown in the Black Sea now?" he says again. "Last time you wanted to climb the Carpathian Mountains, now it's suddenly the sea..."

He keeps going over and over the dangers of all places outside of our yard, as he pours himself another glass of wine, then one more. My mother notices.

"I thought you said you bought that wine for the soccer game."

"It's for the warm up right before the game," my father responds to her, half-jokingly.

Then he turns toward me and lists all the terrible dangers he rescued me from, by not letting me go on any expedition, camp or trip with our class. Last year, I safely stayed at home while my colleagues went for a two week summer camp in the mountains. During Christmas holidays, my class went on a two-day trip to the Moldavian Monasteries. I stayed at home again. My father has always been extra careful about potential dangers. He forbade me to skate, because I could break my legs. He once fell from a bicycle, so I was forbidden to even come close to anything on two wheels. Swimming was an absolute no, because once he saw a child who drowned while walking through a river, when he, my father, was a child himself.

"Well, if I took the first prize," I turn toward my mom who now irons dad's shirts on the kitchen table..."if I took the first prize ....Mrs. Popescu said the one who takes the first prize could go for free to the summer camp...one child per class..."

"Don't even bother," says my father, taking a sip from his glass, "you are not going to the seaside with twenty crazy kids, get that thought out of your mind..."

But I cannot. I keep thinking about it day and night, and I imagine myself getting the first prize, wearing the little crown made of fresh flowers that every first prizewinner gets to wear during the prize awarding ceremony, and then getting on that train for the Black Sea.

The Black Sea...

But then, I don't know how realistic this first prize story is; even I have trouble believing it. For one thing, I know my chances of getting the first prize are really hurt by the six in reading. Secondly, my math notes are not great either. But against my better judgment, the thought that for two weeks I could be far away seeing THE SEA holds me under its spell with such intensity that I cannot stop thinking about it. I am totally crazed by this idea, although a few days later my mother takes me aside and again tells me that even if I took the first prize, my father will still not let me go to the seaside because I am only ten years old. "Things happen," she says. "Look how that crazy boy pushed you on the street. You could have broken your neck and remained handicapped for life. Look how your classmate Marin died playing with other children. Let it go," my mother says, "you'll grow up, you have enough time to see the Black Sea, there is time, there is plenty of time in front of you...you are only ten years old..."

If it doesn't kill you when you are sick...

What I dream is very different from what I see around me when I'm awake. What I dream has mostly to do with shapes: long threads of color twisted into complicated tunnels through which I travel with amazing speed, while seeing, here and there, for a second, little bits from the other reality, the one all of us live in. Those bits and pieces can be anything: the upper part of aunt Aneta's cheek, my friend's voice singing a song, a piece of dry bark, a fly buzzing in circles in an empty room. These bits and pieces are, perhaps, part of some long-forgotten story that I may never remember. But curiously, simple and anonymous as they are, these bits make up the variety of my dreams, because what's a constant night by night are those threads and the twisted shapes that, like clay in the hands of a skilled sculptor, can become anything.

"Silviaaaa..." says Mrs. Popescu. "Wakeee uuup!"

Automatically I turn my head toward the desk where Mrs. Popescu sits, and it is the brusque, startled response of the muscles of my neck, rather than my mind realizing it, that allows me to understand that Mrs. Popescu has caught me in the act.

"What were you dreaming about...?"

Everyone in the class laughs.

"You've must've seen something very interesting in that window because you've been watching it for some time now...."

"I wasn't dreaming," I respond, with the most dignified tone I can master.

That doesn't help, because the class keeps laughing.

"Very well, then, maybe you want to answer the question I just asked... Go ahead."

I didn't hear her asking any question. Actually, I didn't hear anything around me for a while. I try a trick.

I let a few seconds pass, as if I'm thinking about it, and say:

"I don't know."

But she's not letting it go so easily.

"You don't know *what*," says Mrs. Popescu.

"I...don't know the answer to...the question."

Mrs. Popescu smiles.

"Do you know the question? Repeat the question for me."

I lower my chin and shake my head.

"Well, why don't you try harder to pay attention in class instead of dreaming...Otherwise, I'll have to tell your father that you like watching out the window more than paying attention in class. Sit down now."

I do. I swallow hard and strengthen my back. I am going to show Mrs. Popescu that I can be attentive so she doesn't tell my father. Because if that happens, the first thing my father will do is to take away my books with tales. He's deeply convinced that those books *intoxicate* my mind.

"So, Mrs. Popescu asks the class, which is the capital of England?"

Many hands.

"Maria."

"London," says Maria, standing up.

"Very good. The capital of USSR?"

This one everyone knows. There are many hands. Nedelcu, who's repeating the class for the third time, is chosen.

He takes his time to stand up, and when he's done unwinding himself, you can see how tall he is. He looks almost like a man. He takes his time to deliver his words, proudly.

"Mos-cow," says Nedelcu, slowly.

"Good. The capital of Czechoslovakia!"

I raise my hand, fast.

"Silvia."

"Prague! And Prague is the city where Kafka lived," I add, as quickly as I can.

Mrs. Popescu looks at me, long.

"Where did you hear about Kafka?"

"From my friend Ana," I explain.

"Do you know who Kafka is," Mrs. Popescu asks half jokingly. Her tone walks the fine line between curiosity and incredulity.

"A writer," I say. "But I haven't read him."

When I say that, Mrs. Popescu bursts out laughing. Now, that's a first. No one, none of us has ever made Mrs. Popescu laugh. We all see her smiling - a lot - but laughing like this, never. She rests her chin in her palm, while her tone - her face still smiling - becomes serious. She looks long at me and says, in a gentle tone:

"You haven't read him, hm? Oh, Silvia, you really are something..."

Then she laughs again.

"Children, Kafka was a great writer. Many people, adult people, that is - have trouble understanding him because he is a difficult, complex writer. I don't think you should worry about reading his books right now, Silvia...You must be the only child in Bacau to know that there is a writer named Kafka...your parents should be proud of you..."

Now that turned out pretty good. I smile. I look at my friend Duck and she returns my smile, arching her eyebrows admiringly, as if saying: "Don't you say!" But as I think about what Mrs. Popescu said about my parents...well...that I don't know, to be honest. I don't think they are too proud of me. My father believes that my brain has been hijacked by the nonsense I read about every day, such as all those tales with princes, flying horses and faraway lands. He keeps telling me that I'd better learn the multiplication table with nine instead of reading lies all day long or listening to the junk *babeta* (that is, *old hag*) Ana is pouring into my tender mind every time I go to buy bors. My mother would probably raise her eyebrows, frowning, to remind me that it doesn't amount to much that I know some writer's name as long as I have six in reading. And I know she's right: how am I going to get the first prize and go to seaside when I have a six in reading and an eight in math? And others (my colleagues Maria and Liza included) have ten all over? Plus, my parents do not do any favors for Mrs. Popescu. For example, Nedelcu's mother brings Mrs. Popescu cheese made from sheep's milk and the enemy's mother, Mrs. Lazar, who is a hairdresser, trims and styles Mrs. Popescu's hair. And Mrs. Stroe, Maria's mother, brings Mrs. Popescu delicacies such as Nescafe and even other expensive and difficult to find things like Guban shoes.

"Let's go back to our geography lesson, shall we? Who knows what is the capital of France?"

Everyone raises a hand, happy to show off. We go through three or four more questions, when the bell's sound fills the classroom with its heavenly sound. Break time! In a few seconds, we are all out in the schoolyard, a huge fenced area covered with asphalt and swarming with pupils running, walking, talking, yelling. As we get out, Duck takes me aside in a little shady area behind one of school's corners. We are alone. There, she pulls a little bottle from her pocket. It is filled with an opaque pink liquid.

"What is it? Let me see."

Duck hands me the bottle. On the label, which is written in a foreign language, I can see a name in large capital letters: "Nistroprophan solution." Above it, and partially covering the original label, there is another label on which is written in Romanian: "*A se lua numai la indicatia medicului.*" "By prescription only."

"I don't understand. It's a drug. It says here. By prescription only."

"It's raspberry syrup," says Duck.

"Cannot be. Don't you see here? It's some kind of drug."

"Yes, it's a drug, but it's in raspberry syrup. It's very good. I had a teaspoon this morning. Do you wanna try it?"

She opens the bottle and passes it under my nose.

Oh, my God. It smells like heaven. It smells better than heaven.

"It smells really good. Where did you get it?"

"Grandma got it; it is a gift from a nurse who works at the orphanage. They've got some medicine from France and the nurse gave grandma two bottles, in case my brother or I get a cold. It is for cold, but it cannot kill you if you drink a little, right? If it doesn't kill you when you are sick, it cannot kill you when you are healthy, right?"

Now, I have to admit, she has a point. And it just smells way too good. And besides, it's a medicine; it's supposed to be good for you, right?

"Wanna try it?" Duck says. "I'll have some."

When she smells it again, her face relaxes into an expression of total delight. She drinks in gulps, twice. A third of the bottle is gone. She smacks her lips.

"Mt-mt-mt. Very gooood. French stuff."

I take the bottle and carefully test it on the tip of my tongue. If the smell was good, the taste is a thousand times better. It is so flavorful that I take two gulps myself before I give it back to Duck.

"I told you," she says, looking into my eyes.

She drinks one more mouthful. I take it and drink again.

"Ooooooooo!" she says. "My turn!"

I give it back to her. It's not a big bottle. When she turns it up to drink the last drop, the bell rings again. The bottle is empty now, but when we walk to class we feel like we are floating. I still have in my mouth the wonderful taste of raspberry syrup. Not even the least hint of bitterness. The raspberry syrup you buy from the grocery store doesn't stand a chance compared to this wonderful French syrup.

Next hour is history, and we learn about the National Day of Romania, August the 23rd.

"The liberation day was possible," says Mrs. Popescu, "when our army, along with the army of our great friend to the east, USSR, won decisive victories against the enemies, in particular against the Germans. On August 23, 1944, our country became a free country. You should be very proud of the sacrifices that our soldiers, our great army made to free our country from the Nazis. And you should feel very good about the wonderful progress made by our country since the Second World War. In only 24 years, the Communist Party has become the most important force in our society. It is a matter of great pride, children, to become a member of the Communist Party. All this remarkable progress - rebuilding our country after the war, building new factories, new plants, schools and free manuals for pupils like you, building hospitals for sick people - all these could not have been possible without the most important layer of our society, the working class. You should all feel very good about your parents who are workers in the factories, in the plants. About people who, with their bare hands, built the society of today. You should feel good," continues Mrs. Popescu...

I should feel good, but I don't. My stomach feels heavy and I am a bit dizzy. I have troubles concentrating and following Mrs. Popescu. I look at Duck. She looks quite all right.

"Do you feel OK?" I ask her in a low voice.

"Oh, yes," she says, with bright eyes and two round red spots on her cheeks.

She turns her head to Mrs. Popescu who explains that next year the best pupils in our class will become pioneers. She tells us about it:

"Children, it is a great honor to be a pioneer. At the beginning of our next school year, the best of you will become members of the Pioneer Organization. You will wear a special uniform: navy blue pants or skirts, white shirts and the red tie *cravata*."

I like pioneers' uniform. In particular I like the red *cravata*. A cravata is a triangular scarf, made of red nylon that you wear on your shoulders and back. One corner of the triangle rests on your back. Its front two corners are passed through a tiny transparent ring and become a little red tie under your neck.

I walk home thinking about the pioneer uniform. I am very anxious to become a pioneer. I hope I'll be among the first ones in our class to become a pioneer. Wearing new clothes, instead of our daily uniform, seems exciting and I keep thinking about it as I slowly make it to my house, scratching my arms. In particular my left arm itches. When I pull my sleeve up, I see a big red spot on my left elbow. It is very itchy and very red.

As soon as I enter the door, my mother takes a look at me and almost shouts: "What on earth has happened to you?"

"Nothing."

"What do you mean nothing? Come here!"

Mom takes me by the window and looks at me. She gently touches my cheeks.

"You've got an allergy, something...Does it itch?"

I acknowledge by scratching.

"Don't scratch, don't! This is no joke; we have to go to the polyclinic. I'll ask aunt Aneta to take care of Mirela until your father comes home...Are you hungry?" she asks.

"No, I'm not hungry. I don't feel so good, mom. My stomach hurts."

"I'll dress and we leave immediately," mom says.

While she dresses, I go in the next room and look in the round wall mirror. Now I see why my mother shouted. Like a tropical fish, I'm covered by countless bright red spots on my cheeks, my forehead, my neck. I even have one on the tip of my nose. Not to speak about those itchy ones on my arms and belly.

We leave Mirela with aunt Aneta. I don't want to enter Aneta's house, but mom makes me.

"Look at her," mom says to Aneta. "Have you ever seen something like this?"

Aneta pulls me by the window and inspects my face in great detail, without saying anything.

"What did you eat today?" my mother asks. "The sandwich I made you this morning was fresh...I made one for everyone, we all ate the same..."

"Ah, I know! You walked through nettle, didn't you?" Aneta says, suddenly illuminated. "Tell the truth!"

"No, what nettle," I snap back, "I was at school!"

"Let's go," mother says, taking my hand. "Be good," she says to Mirela, and kisses her on her cheek. On our way to the polyclinic, mom talks to me continuously to distract me from scratching myself. Finally we are there.

"It's good we see the doctor now, and not in the morning. In the morning this polyclinic it's so crowded you can't throw a needle in."

And indeed, mom is right. The waiting room in front of Doctor Vale's office is empty. Well, almost. There are only two other people there, patiently waiting on the old vinyl chairs. And the two people are, of course, Duck - her face covered by big red spots - and her mother, Mrs. Neamtu.

Mrs. Neamtu is a blond woman with short hair and lots of freckles on her face. She would be almost beautiful (because she has white skin and large green eyes) if she didn't have such a mean heart. I don't like her, and I don't like Duck's father either: they both are wicked people who spend all their mornings and evenings (during day time they both go to work) quarreling and blaming one another for their miserable lives; and, from time to time, beating their children. They even smack Adrian, their three-year old son who's handicapped and doesn't know what's happening around him. Now, as I see Mrs. Neamtu, I know Duck and I are in trouble. We both have the same red spots all over our skin. When she sees us, Mrs. Neamtu stands up and watches me attentively, as I open my mouth to say, "Good afternoon."

"Hi, Silvia," she responds, still looking long at me.

My mother comes by Duck's chair and pats her head:

"Look at you too," she says. "What did you two do today?"

"Nothing," Duck responds, quickly.

She then sits on her red chair, tight lipped and looking mostly on the floor. Only when she must look at my mother she raises her eyes for a second. In the next second, she's watching the floor again. Or the walls. She does not look at her mother when Mrs. Neamtu says or asks her something. She responds quickly, keeping her face turned away. This would never occur if she were my mother's daughter. Since we were small children, my mother took great care to make sure my sister and I looked into the eyes of the person we speak to. "Look into the eyes of the person you speak to, not at the walls. You are not talking to the walls." This worked out so well that some people are uncomfortable with me. For example, when I first went to buy bors from Crina and Ana, I looked so intensely at them (into their eyes and at their brown spots too) that Crina couldn't take it anymore and told me to stop staring like a monkey at her. I mumbled something and blushed. Since, I tried to look just into her eyes: but I must confess that her brown spots exert a magnetic fascination to me. Now, I wonder what people on the street must've thought as I walked back and forth covered in red spots like some exotic creature. Moreover, Duck and I must make a nice picture as we sit, both of us, on red chairs, in front of Doctor Vale's office.

My mother talks with Mrs. Neamtu about Adrian. They talk in a low voice, a few feet away, but I hear them saying: "wets the bed," "can not feed himself," "God wanted to punish me." I know that Adrian brings great pain to that household. When I went last week to Duck's house and I opened the window, Duck started screaming at me so hard that I dropped the apple I had in my left hand. We were inside her living room. I had only wanted some fresh air.

"Close that, now!" yelled Duck. I stood up to close it, but she was faster. In a second, she came by the window and smacked it closed as if she was desperately trying to repair an irreparable ill that had just occurred. I retrieved my apple from the floor and stood there, not knowing if I should go and wash the apple or wait to see what she did next. I decided to wait for her to calm down.

"Yesterday Adrian tried to jump out of the window," Duck said. "My mom said that if I forget and leave the window open and he runs away and kills himself, she will kill me too, with her own hand!"

Now, because our mothers are a few feet away, I whisper to Duck:

"Did you tell her?"

"What?"

"...about the syrup...did you tell her why we got the spots?"

"No, no! If she finds out that I stole the syrup bottle, she'll beat me...don't tell...say they just appeared like that!"

"On both of us? At once?"

"Yeees! So what!?"

"You know what?" I say. "We can say it appeared from nettle! You know, when we walked home...we walked through nettle...by the Jewish cemetery..."

I raise my eyes to the ceiling. God bless aunt Aneta for coming up with this!

"Aaaa! That's good! That's very good!"

The doctor's door opens and the nurse says:

"Come in, girls! Come in!"

We stand up, and slowly make it into doctor's office. Our mothers follow.

The doctor is an old woman with a large wrinkled face and grayish hair. She's writing something in a large book, but in a few seconds she's done. She raises her eyes toward the two of us, then comes close to us.

"All right, what do we have here? What is the problem?"

"Aaa...today...we walked through nettle...and.. we got these spots..." says Duck, as if reciting a poem.

The doctor touches her face, feels the spots on her cheek, then on my arms. Her touch is soft and calming, like a grandmother's touch.

"When exactly did they appear?"

"At noon."

"Are they all over the body?"

She looks at our legs, which are as well decorated with itchy red spots.

"Yes. Everywhere, I say."

"You two are friends?"

"Yes," I respond. "We are in the same class."

"I see. Does it itch all the time, or does it stop and start only if you scratch it?"

"All the time," we respond.

"What did you eat today?"

"Aaa, sandwich," Duck responds.

"Anything else?"

"No."

"Did you take any medication? Any pill?"

"No," we respond with one voice.

"Well, I'll tell you what...these do not look like nettle eczema... because these spots are well circumscribed, see? Round...no irregular margins...but you may have some allergic reaction to something you touched or ate...and, anyway, from now on make sure you stay away from nettle, yes?"

"Yes, yes," we both say in a chorus.

The doctor looks at our mothers.

"I'll give them some anti-allergy pills. Buy them on your way home. And take two per day for five days, yes? Understood?"

"Thank you, Mrs. Doctor," our mothers say.

While she writes prescriptions, we look at one another, relieved. Our mothers take the prescriptions, we say thank you again and leave the room. Freedom! Liberty! We made it!

As we walk out of the polyclinic Duck's mother comes close to us.

"Why did you walk through nettle?"

She doesn't wait for an answer but smacks Duck's head with her palm.

"What did I tell you about coming straight home from school?"

Duck recoils, and bursts into tears.

"Mrs. Neamtu, please, don't beat the child...she is a sick child, for God's sake," mother says. "Please!"

"Oh, Mrs. Marcu, you don't know how she makes my life bitter. What were you doing in nettle when I always tell you to come home directly from school?"

"Eh, now...what she did does not deserve this...please, she doesn't feel good, don't you see?"

"She feels good, all right, I saw the two of them grinning when they got out of the doctor's office!"

"But to beat her...she does not deserve that..."

"All right, I didn't kill her, did I?" Mrs. Neamtu says, and unexpectedly, pulls Duck toward her breast with her left hand. Although I expected Duck would try to run away, she doesn't. She lets herself be led by her mother. She doesn't say a word. She still has tears in her eyes.

"We'd better take the bus on our way home after we stop at the pharmacy," says mom. "Good bye, now," she waves to Duck and her mother, who cross the street to go to a relative who lives nearby.

"Good bye, Duckie," I say, and wave as well. Mother keeps saying, as we walk home from the bus stop:

"This Mrs. Neamtu...sometimes I don't understand certain people..."

"And she beats her with a leather belt if Duck gets a mark lower than seven," I say. "They beat her with a leather belt, both her parents! Duck told me!"

"See? Now I recall you got a six in reading, didn't you? Have to check out that leather belt your father has....when we get home..."

"Moooom!!" I shake her hand.

She laughs, and caresses my hair.

A few seconds pass.

"By the way," mother says, "I thought you said you didn't walk through nettle today..."

"Oh...we..actually...we...did walk...a little bit..." I say, carefully. "Just a bit."

"Just a bit, ha?" mother says, opening the gate of our fence.

She laughs as she enters the house.

"You'd better lay in the bed," says mom. "Here, take your pill." She brings me water:

"Drink all this. I'll make you a linden tea, so you can sleep a little. Are you hungry?"

I say no. And she nods, kindly:

"Go and lay in the bed, Silvia."

I have a headache. I go and open the cupboard door. When opened, the door forms a screen that creates some privacy. I go behind that door, take my blouse and shirt off and put on my pajamas. When I close the door, I notice that there is chalk on its the lower left corner: a little castle with three towers and an animal with four legs (cat, dog?) that my sister has sketched with yellow chalk. I open my mouth to tell mom (just yesterday mom told Mirela for a hundredth time to stop writing on the furniture, "I brought you pencils and a drawing pad, see?") but I give it up at the last second. I close the door, returning the castle and the four-legged creature back to the darkness of the cupboard.

I sneak under the blanket in bed. I feel very tired. My skin doesn't itch anymore. Instead, I feel a slight pain when I touch it, even slightly, with the tip of my fingers. I lay on my back, and feel every bit of my body burning, as if hundreds of little creatures move underneath my skin and bite here and there. I find a position less painful, on my left side, and watch mom preparing the tea. She makes linden tea using flowers from the linden tree that grows in my grandmother's yard. It is an old, majestic linden whose flowers, when in bloom, smell like a dream. My mother has water boiling in a pan. She opens a small white cloth bag and takes a pinch of florettes. I hear the dry, papery noise the flowers make when rustled by her fingers. She places them in the water and in less than a minute the whole kitchen fills with the dizzying aroma of linden. Mother pours the tea in a cup, and comes close to me. She puts it close to me, on a little table nearby.

"It's too hot. Wait for a few minutes."

By now I am completely dizzy. Mom caresses my forehead with her palms, gently. I like my mother's hands. Her hands are the most beautiful hands in the world. Nothing, I feel, can ever come close to my mother's hands. Her skin is soft and warm. And no touch is or will ever be - now, years later, ever - as sweet and soothing as the touch of my mother's hand on my forehead. My mother caresses my hair, my cheeks, and says, in a sweet tone:

"What a silly little girl mom has... Does it still hurt?"

And mom smiles at me, and I close my eyes, because I know she's right. And her caress feels so good.

I tighten my eyes even harder and pretend it actually hurts a lot so she will caress me a little longer. She describes circles with her fingers on my face, one cheek, then another, and with my eyes closed I dream I am a shiny stone surrounded by shiny water, like I once saw in my grandmother's village. In my dream, water comes from all directions and surrounds the stone, in slow layers intersected by the afternoon sun.

When I wake up (not fully, having just half of my brain listening to what's going on around me, and the other half still under the clouds of medication) I hear commotion around me. Mom pulls a blazer from the edge of a chair, and my father, sitting on a chair, holds my sister Mirela on his lap. Mirela, in turn, tries to escape, beats the air with her hands and legs and starts yelling, quite loudly. I raise my head. Dad is now trying to hold Mirela's head straight, so mom (now holding a little rectangular mirror towards Mirela's face) attempts to see something with it.

"What's going on," I mumble.

No one responds. Instead, Mirela starts yelling even harder when mom touches her nose, and dad says:

"Mirela, stay still! Stay still when I say!"

Mirela doesn't even consider his words and starts screaming. Tears fall down her cheeks.

"Don't make her cry! Now I can't see anything!"

She holds a handkerchief in her left hand and keeps telling Mirela:

"Mirela, blow your nose when I tell you, sweetie, will you? Please do as I say, listen to mom!"

Mirela doesn't listen and doesn't seem to hear anything. She cries now with long sobs, and starts coughing.

Mom says:

"Got to go to the doctor with this one too. Come on, let's go! I can't pull it out."

Then she turns toward me.

"Silvia, go back to sleep. We have to go to the doctor with Mirela. She pushed a linden flower through her nostril and now it's stuck there."

Some more commotion till father, mom and Mirela leave: *Did you take money, this, that.* Mirela has stopped crying and holds her fingers over her left nostril, where the linden flower has taken residence.

"Breath with your mouth!" says mom. "Open up and breathe with your mouth, honey, yes?"

Mirela acknowledges this with tears in her eyes. A few minutes later I don't see them anymore, as my mind fills with the shadows of the afternoon, in the form of fantastic creatures cast by the trembling light on the kitchen walls.

Ninetimesfouristhirtysix

A week later, the red spots are gone. All I have now are faint speckles, which my mom says will go away in no time. I finally told her why we got the spots - she kept asking me so many times that finally I couldn't stand it anymore and confessed. But I made her swear never to tell Mrs. Neamtu, because that woman will beat Duck with a leather belt if she finds out that Duck stole the cough syrup from her grandmother's cupboard.

"Well," mother says a few moments later, "sooner or later her grandmother will notice that the bottle is gone, you know!"

I raise my eyes from my book. I know that, and I don't know what to respond. I open my mouth and then close it soundlessly, like a fish. Then I go back to my

119

math book. I spent all the time I stayed home rehearsing the multiplication table with 9. That's what I'm doing now. I sit in the bed, propped against a huge pillow and recite, while mother moves around cooking, or cleaning or straightening a drawer:

"Nine times four is thirty-six." "Nine times four is thirty-six." "Nine times four is thirty-six." "Nine times five is forty-five." "Nine times five is forty-five." "Nine times five is forty-five. "

I say it a few times, hoping it will get stuck to my mind forever. Like those insects I saw in the Museum of Natural History, forever attached to some cardboard and looking back at me with huge, empty dead eyes from beneath a glass case. However, words don't behave the same way. They keep floating around in my head and keep becoming other words, over and over. So I decide that the solution to this is to learn by heart a few, such as nine times four is thirty-six, nine times seven is sixty-three and nine times nine is eighty-one. Then, I figure, I can make up the others by adding nine to any of these. This way, I will be able to move up and down on this torturous table as I please and when someone quizzes me, I don't stare back blankly like an insect pinned to a piece of cardboard.

So I say "nine times six is thirty-six" five times. This is when I notice something remarkable: ninetimesfouristhirtysix becomes a sequence of letters and like in a story, boom! there is no meaning left in those words. Ninetimesfouristhirtysix. Ninetimesfouristhirtysix. Ninetimesfouristhirtysix. Ninetimesfouristhirtysix. All I get in my head is the picture of a far away landscape in which the consonants are a zig-zag of sounds that have escaped the tyranny of meaning. Now this I have not seen before! It feels like I liberated words of some burden, I transported them, with my own mind, into a larger space, where no constraints of any kind apply. I stop, deeply surprised, then a few seconds later I do it with nine times five is thirty-six. And it works again. Ninetimesfiveisthirtysix ninetimesfiveisthirtysix ninetimesfiveisthirtysix ninetimesfiveisthirtysix. I say it about six time times, loudly. My mother, who just came from the other room, hears me:

"What are you saying there?

I don't stop because if I stop, the effect is gone. I continue even faster until my mother comes near my bed, gently puts her hand on my mouth and says:

"Stop! You sound like a broken record! What's wrong with you?"

"Father said yesterday that if I learn the multiplication table he will let me go to the camp."

"Yes, I understand this, but don't you think about what you are saying? Nine times five is not thirty-six."

I am too preoccupied with the special effects I created by doing two things at once, learning the table and making words disappear in a magical space, to start arguing. Plus, as I stopped repeating it as a parrot and started talking with my mother, the words came back to life. Air and life filled them out into well known shapes.

"Yes, I know," I respond to my mother, "but I am just getting used to repeating the same thing over and over."

Mother looks at me like you look at a bug. She feels my forehead.

"Do they still itch?"

"No, not at all. The itch is gone."

"You don't have fever, but clearly you are not OK. Why don't you stop for a few moments? Go out and take some fresh air."

What she is asking is inconceivable.

"I am not stopping," I say. "I have to keep repeating these. Father said that if I learn the multiplication by heart and I know it perfectly when he quizzes me, he'll let me go to camp."

"No, he didn't say he will let you go to camp. He said he may let you go to camp."

"Even so," I mumble. "If I stop, then I don't learn, and if I don't learn then I don't have even the slightest chance…"

"Yes, I know, but don't you see that what you are saying doesn't make any sense anymore?"

"I am not stopping," I repeat, slowly, so she can really understand. "Because if I stop, I won't learn it, and if I don't learn it, father will not allow me to go to camp."

Mother doesn't say anything for a few seconds.

"You want that much to go to that camp."

Oh, how sweet her words are. I want that not more, but thousand and thousand of billions of times more than anything on this earth to go to camp. I want to go there so much that I could become a bird and fly there, and when I'll see the Black Sea, I'll fly in circles above it, up, up in the highest sky. I want to go and touch the salty waters, to look at the waves over and over and over. I feel the weight of the foam, delicate and salty on my skin, riding toward the shore like I've seen in movies.

"Take a break anyway," mother says. "I'll speak with your father, maybe-maybe we can find a way to let you go BUT" - she doesn't even pause between the sentences - "BUT this doesn't mean I am promising you a thing! It may be a no, understand? It may be a big fat no. Don't get too excited. We'll see tomorrow. Now, stop this nonsense and go out. Get some fresh air. You've been too long inside this house."

"I am going to see Duck," I say, placing the books by the bed.

"Go and see Duck, very well. Make sure the two of you don't drink some silly syrup again."

"No, don't worry," I say, putting on my pants and a blouse. I go out the door in a big rush because suddenly I have the most excellent idea of how to solve the two problems of my life, going to camp and learning the multiplication table, with one smart move. Killing, as father says, two rabbits with one stone. And I am sure Duck will be interested in joining me, oh, yes, she will!

Duck lives very close, at the end of our street. Her family occupies the two end rooms of a very long row of houses. The other end of that house I have never seen, because it is engulfed by large trees and bushes into some kind of jungle Duck and I were told never to come close to. I knock at Duck's door. I so hope her parents are not at home. She opens the door:

"Silvia! Come in!"

"You alone?"

Duck smiles.

"Yep! Mom took the day off and went with Adrian to aunt Magda."

"Why didn't you go?"

"Well, 'cause she thinks that maybe my spots may still be contagious, you know!"

She lets me in. Her house is as simple as ours and each room contains just the bare essentials: a bed, a table, two cupboards, chairs. Her windows have the thin, transparent curtains with designs of leaves falling in all directions, just as our windows do. And as do half of the houses of Bacau, I suppose: it is one of the two kinds of curtains you can buy in the town anyway.

"What were you doing?"

"Nothing," says Duck.   "I was reading the multiplication table. It won't get into my head."

"Know what? Mom said that she would talk with my father to let me go to the camp - to the seaside - but I don't know if he'll say yes. So here's my idea: let's go to church and pray. I'll pray to God that my parents let me go to the seaside and that I remember the multiplication table with nine. And you can do the same, pray you'll remember what you learned today, what do you say?"

Duck considers.

"We can go to the Precista church, yeees," she says, and from her tone I see she likes the idea. "Yeees!"

It doesn't take too long to arrive at the church, a grand building with three grand spires each extending a tall cross toward the sky. Around the church there is a large cemetery with white, gray, and black stone crosses and, here and there, some grand, imposing marble crosses, among green bushes and rows of flowers. There is no one in front of the church or in the cemetery - it is noon, on Thursday - but as we enter the church, we see two women kneeling in front of icons, against opposite walls.

The first thing about churches is the smell, of course. There are candles burning everywhere, and being rather dark - the church has huge windows painted with saints riding horses, so not a lot of light comes through - the little light from the candles flickers and illuminates the saints' faces in an eerie way. They look at us from every corner of the church with elongated, skeletal faces and big eyes full of remorse.

"Let's light a candle," whispers Duck as we step in and pass by a large table with many trays of sand on which there are stuck countless burning candles. Their stems are yellow, and thin as crayons are, and about twice as long. On a chair nearby there is a bunch of new ones. We each take one and bring the wick close to a burning candle. The fire engulfs the fresh wick with a solemn, articulate flame. Holding the candle and walking in small steps, I go around the left wall, looking at all those icons.

I can see the name of each saint, painted directly on the wall, and although the letters belong to some kind of old-fashioned alphabet, they still bear resemblance to the letters we learned in school. Duck follows me, with her candle in her hand as well. We walk rather slowly along the walls, crossing ourselves now and then. As we move along, we come close to one of the old women kneeling in front of a huge portrait of Virgin Mary with the baby

Jesus in her arms. I like that picture a lot. I like her large, black eyes looking at me no matter where I am in the church. The way she holds baby Jesus: detached, almost posing, and most of all I like her hands with their long, thin fingers, holding her son on the top of her palms as the baby seemingly floats on a pillow of air, in a state of irreversible grace. Moreover, if you look closely, baby Jesus is surrounded by many little clouds that float around him like bubbles of soap. The woman crosses herself, then raising her head she looks at us. Her face shows warmth and kindness.

"God may have you in his mercy, little girls," she says. "God bless you for coming to the holy church to pray. Nowadays you never see children coming to the holy church."

When she crosses herself again, she smiles to both of us and thus opens a large mouth with no teeth in sight. Just red gums, beyond wrinkled lips. I automatically cross myself and keep walking along the wall, and only after we pass the old lady Duck looks at me and I look at her. I snort, softly. Then we turn again toward the walls and look at the painted saints. Saint Nicholas fighting the three-headed monster. Archangel Michael, his face austere and withdrawn, slightly resembling Mr. Gogu. The church is silent, and feels even more so when all these eyes follow our every move from every spot on the wall. Duck, who's now toward the opposite corner of the church, where the other old lady prays, starts coughing. Then she stops, and coughs again, faintly. And then one more time. That's a signal. I cross the middle of the church toward an open space with a long table with many large silver crosses, icons and burning candles. I stop for a second to stick my candle in the sand like Duck just did and come close to her. We are now very close to the old lady who didn't seem to notice us and was praying fervently since we entered the church. Duck stands in front of a wall with smaller paintings. Many of them are scenes, rather than portraits. We see Jesus followed by a flock of sheep; and then another scene where many people look at fish dropping from Jesus' hands. Below those two, there is something really small, so small that we both have to kneel to observe it.

It is a scene from hell. First, we can see flames burning in long tongues, dark yellow flames blackened here and there by the smoke of the church, and above those flames, we can see sinners scrambling to get out, somewhere up into a dark cloud of smoke and dust where some luckier ones already are. Their faces show bewilderment and remorse, and look imploringly toward long columns of smoke that seem to have two horns and a tail.

"Look at this!" Duck points.

In the lower left corner of that icon, the painter did a little devil, so little you can barely see it. We really have to look carefully to see all the details. The little devil has a twisted tail with a tuft of hair toward its end and two large generous ears, instead of horns, that look exactly like enemy's ears! Moreover, there is a speckle on top of his head that makes it look like there is a band covering his head.

"Florin!" I say and in the same second we both burst into laugher. In the silent church our voices resonate unexpectedly loud, and when we look up all those saints look back. Duck is the first to stop laughing and jostles me:

"SSShhht! Shut up! Shut up!"

I cannot stop. It is not only the ears, the head and the bully attitude that so well say enemy all over, but also the fact that this little devil attempts, with his right hand, to impale a sinner with something whose size and shape resemble too well a kitchen fork. This is even more ridiculous and I keep laughing. Duck jostles me with her left arm.

"Shut up at once! Don't you hear me! It's a sin!"

The old lady who is praying close to us raises her head and says:

"What are you two doing here in the sacred house of God? What do you think this is, a playground?"

The more she talks, the more I cannot stop. I feel bad, and now I have tears in my eyes, but the more I try to stop, the harder I laugh.

"That's enough! Out! Out with both of you! It's a sin to laugh in the church! Get out!"

"But she didn't mean..." says Duck, already standing up.

The old lady doesn't want to hear it:

"Out! What are you doing here at this hour anyway? Why aren't you in school?"

"Let's go," says Duck.

I stand up and follow Duck, trying to maintain a straight face. When we are out, we stop for a second to breathe in the fresh air. It feels so good.

"Stop it! See what you did?? Now where can we pray? That witch!"

She is sad, and I am sorry.

131

"Sorry Duckling, I didn't mean to..."

"Did you at least pray?"

"No," I respond. "Did you?"

"No, I didn't. And I know you didn't mean to spoil everything, but now we didn't pray, and tomorrow we have this quiz, and if I get a bad mark..."

I am sad too. I didn't get to say even a word in my mind about my most important wish, going to the summer camp. I got all carried away by all those paintings and by that little devil.

We walk a few steps.

"You know what," I say. "Let's go and pray in the Catholic Church. There is one nearby."

"But we are orthodox, not catholic. We cannot pray in the wrong church."

"Yes, I know," I respond, "but if you think about it, a church is a church, right? And besides, I have never been in a Catholic Church, have you?"

She shakes her head.

"See? There are lots of people who pray to the Catholic God, so he must be a good God, right? And because he's good, then he'll listen to us too, right?"

"He should," agrees Duck. "Ok, let's go and pray there. But once we are there," says Duck, "you also have to pray to be forgiven that you laughed in this church, promise?" As we walk there, she also tells me that perhaps we should consider praying twice as hard in the Catholic Church, as we are kind of foreigners there and we want to be sure that we are being heard and considered.

In a few minutes we are there. The Catholic Church, named St. Nicholas, is huge, at least tree times larger than the Orthodox Church.

The difference between them, I feel, is the difference between the wooden dolls that my grandfather made for me when I was three years old and the expensive ones that my parents bought for me from the toy shop. The wooden ones were rudimentary, straightforward and strangely exotic in the way their linear anatomy was revealed to me. They were so different from the mass produced ones, which were made of rubber, colorful and so detailed that I almost thought of them as of miniature people. I liked the rubber ones a lot, I still do, to a certain extent, but can't forget the effort of imagination one had to put in to figure out the wooden dolls (their shoulders, slightly asymmetrical, their stiff legs and hands held at various angles apart from the body.) Or my fascination as I watched my grandfather releasing that promise of a doll from a tree branch. I liked to look long at their smooth faces - no eyes, no mouth, no nose - and imagine a cry, a smile, a scowl. The rubber ones came to me with a standard smile already stamped on their faces, and there the challenge, sometime, was to dismiss that artificial smile. In a parallel way, I feel that the glorious decorum of the Catholic Church overwhelms me with colors, with its massive design, with its sounds.

Duck and I step inside and suddenly something extraordinary happens: it's like we step into a city. Everything is different here: first, the church is full of benches. Brown, polished benches placed in two rows all along the length of the church. There are people sitting on these benches, and a priest at the altar; and also, I see, surprised, a procession of little people - they are boys, I realize, when I look better - bearing something in their hands and walking single file, slowly, around the altar. Boys!? Children? What are they doing there?

"Stop staring like a peasant," says Duck, "and do what these people do!"

Two men enter the church and stop by the door, cross themselves, then touch some liquid in a big silver pot by the door and again cross themselves, touching their foreheads and shoulders with their fingers.

"What is this?" I whisper.

"It's holy water," responds Duck. "I saw this in a movie. Do it."

She crosses herself after she touches the holy water and I do the same. We enter the church and sit in the last two rows of benches. The service is just beginning: the priest speaks slowly, reciting as he moves his hand toward the multitude to bless it. I look around: the walls are full of pictures in bright colors and saints are all happy and quite plump if not fat. Even the horses they ride are fat. The walls resemble a museum rather than the church I am used to. The altar, made of a huge silvery panel on which angels and saints are encrusted, shines under the countless lights of the church.

"Look at your right!" I say slowly to Duck. "Look at that blue saint to your right on the wall: he looks like he has just had a huge breakfast!"

On the wall, a chubby saint, holding a book in his hand, looks back. He is dressed in bright blue clothes and his face is pink and content. He looks like a happy grandfather at peace with his life. His eyes are bright and his fingers plump.

Duck gives me a look so dreadful that I immediately turn and cross myself.

"Pray!" Duck says, slowly, in my ear.

I close my eyes so tightly that I see sparks for a few seconds. It is dark and the noise of the church around me dies away. I let the sparks dissolve slowly and try to think what to tell God. My first impulse is to start like I would start a letter: "God, please..." but then I stop. That's not what God is looking for. What he wants to know is if I really, really want to go to the camp. Really, really, more than anything else in this whole world. I ponder that for a second, and my feelings grow in me with such intensity, such beauty and such power that all I need to do is to hold them there, for a second, for God to see them. He will know. Complete, overwhelming clarity and beauty surround me as I think about going to the sea, about seeing those faraway lands that I know only from tales. I let myself enveloped by this warm and soft feeling. Words, I feel, aren't even needed. This is grace. The seaside. I float.

A few minutes later, I open my eyes and look at Duck. She still has her eyes shut and her face shows concentration and determination, while her lips mumble softly. And then, above us, in large waves that fill this church busy like a bee hive, the organ starts playing. Its sound resonates so powerfully inside this building that my train of thought stops in its tracks, startled. Duck opens her eyes and looks at me:

"What is this?"

Then the choir adds to the organ music and now the church around us is enveloped in layers and layers of majestic sound.

"I didn't finish praying," Duck says, with spite. "I was this close! But you know what? Let's go home. I've had enough church today."

On our way home we talk about the churches we visited. The Orthodox Church - from which the toothless witch threw us out because we laughed – and how much more we like that one. We also discuss if it's possible that someone pokes your ribs with a kitchen fork when you go to hell. We then talk about the Catholic Church, how much more colorful, how much happier those saints were with their pink faces and bright clothes.

"I know why they are so happy!" I say to Duck, just as she enters her yard.

She stops.

"Why?"

"Because," I say, stopping for effect. "Because these catholics come from Rome, right?"

"Yeeees," Duck says.

"Italy? Ha? Got it?"

"No. What?"

"What do people do in Italy? All day long? Mrs. Capellini?"

"What? Pasta?"

"You got it. They prepare pasta and then they eat it! All day long! That's why they are so plump and happy!"

Mrs. Capellini is Duck's next door neighbor who always invites us for pasta when she sees us playing in the yard, outside of Duck's house. She is a large woman with fat legs and a maternal smile all over her face.

I smile back.

"Eh? Capisco?"

"One more word," Duck warns, "and God will take away everything you prayed for today!"

"God is smarter than that. You'll see."

And that was true. Two days later, we both got an eight at the math quiz.

"Not the best, after so much rehearsing and memorizing and praying to God in two churches," I say to Duck on our way back from school that day.

"Well, for one thing we didn't pray in two churches...just in one, as I remember, because someone started laughing...And, the bottom line is, at least we didn't get a seven," Duck says, sighing happily. "God helped us. We should go and pray for our next quiz as well."

"You know what," I say to Duck. "Quite honestly, I don't think this church thing helped at all. I don't think it made the slightest difference. I'm not going to church again to pray for favors."

"What are you going to do instead, then?"

"Oh, I don't know. Want to play thugs and turkeys at Liviu's instead?"

"OK," she says.

An hour later, we go to Liviu's house, where our friends get together to play from time to time. Liviu lives very close to me. We enter a yard full of children running like rabbits all around. As soon as they see us, they start running after us as well, and in an instant we are part of the game, a game we play and understand so much better.

Rat's daughter

My first question to mom, as soon as I arrive home from school the next day, is:

"Did you speak? Did you speak with him? Mom, did you speak with dad?"

She doesn't respond, so I come closer to see what she's doing. Mother is boiling starch in a big pot. She mixes the whitish, cloudy thick liquid with a large wooden spoon, then, a few seconds later, when countless tiny bubbles start popping up, she turns down the stove flame. Then she turns toward me:

"What did you say, Silvia? What?"

I look into her eyes. Deep, deep inside there is a kaleidoscope of lights and sparks, a world that contains the answers to all my questions, even the ones I don't dare ask. Now, I sense warmth in those eyes so dear to me, but I am afraid to be hopeful.

She smiles and nods.

"I can? I can go? I can really, really go?"

"Yes, you can go."

"Father said so?"

"Yes, I talked with him this morning."

I am so happy that I jump to hug her. She almost takes a step back, into the stove and the boiling starch pot.

"Slow down, slow down now!"

She laughs and hugs me, then she keeps me close to her breast and ruffles my hair.

There is too much energy in me. More than I can use by just saying "thank you" which I repeat as a broken record as I jump around the room. I try to sit on a chair. Then I jump up again. I look left and right. This room is small, too small. This whole house is way too small.

"I'm going to tell Duck!" I say, and rush out the door.

"Careful when you cross the street," says mom. "Careful!"

Outside, Mirela sits on the bench underneath the old pear tree licking an oversized candy stuck on a long yellow stick. I come close to her.

"You know what? I am going to the seaside! To the camp! I really am!"

Mirela looks at me, long, and licks her candy one more time.

"I know. Mom told me. And you know what I am going to do when you are at the seaside?"

"No, what?"

"I'll go to grandma's and play with our cousins. And mom will buy me a tableware set for my dolls!"

"Aaa," I say. "This is good! This is very good!"

"A red one, with red forks, and plates, and little glasses," she explains. "Like we saw in the toy store, remember?"

"I'm going to Duck!" I say. "Want to come with me?"

"No," she says, licking her candy again.

Just before I get out of the yard I hear my mother's voice again.

"Silvia, thank God you are still here. Why don't you go and buy some bors from the Lecca sisters on your way back?"

Oh, bors again. I may escape childhood diseases, I may escape even death, I imagine, as extraordinary as that may seem, but bors, never. I'll never ever escape this chore. I imagine myself being ninety nine years old, and the Lecca sisters being at least five hundred fifty years old, and even then, I realize, I will walk back and forth between our houses carrying a raffia bag in my hands. Even then. But I cannot say no. No way can I say no.

"Sure. Give me the bottles."

Out on the street, I plan this little trip in my mind. I'll first go to see Duck. I have to tell her the great news.

As I walk, I inquire: shall I just tell her, directly, or shall I beat around the bush a little bit? Pretend that nothing happened at first. That's a much better strategy. It will make everything so much more interesting.

I knock at her door. When Duck opens the door, I blurt it out:

"Duckie, you know what? I'm going to the seaside camp! Mom and dad are going to let me go to the seaside camp! Mom just told me!"

"Oh, that's good! Good for you!"

She turns her head and then whispers:

"They're all at home!"

"Who, your parents?"

"Yes!"

I sense displeasure in her tone.

"Can you come? With me? To the camp?"

"No, no way!"

From her tone I understand that she never seriously thought that something like that could happen to her. Ever.

145

"Who's there, Claudia? Close that door and go do your homework!"

I hear a voice, her father's, angrily swearing. Then something falling. Then her mother, yelling.

"Because I told you a thousand time," I hear Duck's father yelling, "a thousand time, not less, to put this stupid thing somewhere else! Every time I stumble on the stupid thing!"

"Why don't you open your eyes!" Duck's mother yells, even lauder. "Open those stupid eyes!"

"Got to go," Duck whispers, as she closes the door. "See you tomorrow!"

"Sorry," I mumble.

I take my raffia bag and leave. Such a hell in this house. Every time I come here, her parents quarrel, yell at each other or at Duck and Adrian. I am happy when I am out, out and far from their yard. In a few minutes I knock at Lecca's door. Ana opens it.

"Good afternoon. Mom would like two liters of bors," I say.

"Come in, dear, come in, don't stand there!"

I enter the house, and give her the two bottles and the money, 1 leu.

"How are you," asks Ana.

"Very good! Mom just told me that I am going to the seaside in August! To the camp!"

"I am happy to hear that, dear!" Ana says. "Very happy!"

I look around. Everything is in perfect order in the Lecca house. The table is clean, and uncluttered. The sofa is covered with a neatly arranged blanket. Even the window curtain has all its folds arranged at equal distance one from another. On a little table by the window I see a thin book. I can see the title, TALES. In small letters, the cover page also lists the names of the stories. One of those subtitles catches my attention: The rat's daughter.

"The rat's daughter?" I hear myself asking. "What is that?"

The title sounds so unusual for a story, mostly because all stories I know have to do with dying kings, wrinkled witches or wonderfully beautiful princesses - princesses so beautiful that men who see them instantly lose their minds. But rats? I never thought there could be a story about rats.

"That," says Ana, is a very old story. "Do you want to hear it?"

"Sure!"

"Well, then. Once upon a time," she says, setting the bottle aside and sitting on the chair by the table, and patting the other chair and thus inviting me to sit also, "once upon a time there was a rat. Old rat. So old that the hairs of his eyelashes had turned white a long time ago. And he had a daughter he loved more than anything in this world. And one day, a miraculous thing happened. As he was minding his own business, carrying a piece of carrot to his hole, he saw a stone rolling really fast toward a young rat who was playing near the road. So he rushed over and pushed that other rat away, and thus saved his life. Now, you see - that other rat was none other than the son of the king of rats. And the king immediately sent after him to thank him for saving his son's life.

'Ask me something, anything,' said the king, and it will happen. Because, you see, the king had magical powers. And the old rat thought a bit about it and said:

'Oh, Your Highness, if you really want to do something for me, then make my daughter into a woman, a real human being, so she can live in a better world than I do! Make it so that she never remembers she was born a rat!'

The king asked:

'Are you sure that this is what you want?'

'Yes, Your Highness.'

And the king, with a sign of his hand, transformed the rat's daughter into a beautiful young woman. Looking at her you'd have never guessed she had once been a rat...

Now," Ana continued, "the young woman led a contented life. She married a wonderful man who loved her very much and had three beautiful children. They all lived in a large house and their life was peaceful and pleasant. But one day, what do you think happened?"

I shrug my shoulders and look intensely in Ana's eyes, waiting.

"One day," continues Ana, "as the young woman was picking mushrooms in the woods by her house, she saw something moving in the bushes. She looked closely and looked and looked at that creature. It was a rat. Her blood rushed to her temples and she felt her heart filling with a strange desire. The most bizarre, unexplained desire. Out of nowhere a bittersweet yearning filled her chest, with such power that she thought she was going to die right there on the spot. She fell madly in love with the strange creature and instantly forgot, as if struck by lightning, about her husband and her beautiful children. She started following the rat deeper and deeper into the forest. And as she was following the rat, a strange thing started to happen. She saw how he grew in her eyes with every step, and sensed, as she was trying to catch up with him, the long tail emerging behind her, as she was making her turns, trying to avoid huge stones and branches that were now blocking her way. So," Ana says, standing up and grasping the bors pitcher, "there you have it: Rat's daughter... in spite of her father's wishes, she became what she has always been..."

She then fills my bottle, in silence. In turn, I don't say too much, because this story is too different from any other story I ever heard. But I keep thinking about it, and, on my way back, I try to imagine how it was possible for the king to transform a rat, boom! into a woman of unspeakable beauty. Then, as I take the turn on my street, I stop hit by an unpleasant thought. I look ahead, behind: there is no one around me on the street.

Slowly, twisting my head as much as I can, I look toward my back. To my infinite relief, no tail has emerged. And so I resume my walk, with a slight sigh and a frown on my face, as I keep thinking what this strange story means.

Going to Geneva

It is a bright July morning. My friend Duck and I sit outside on the bench by the old pear tree in my yard. Duck came to return the Chinese Stories book I lent her last week.

"Listen to this," she says. "My own grandfather. It happened last night."

I am curious. Her grandfather does all kinds of crazy things.

"What?"

Right in that second, my father opens the door of our kitchen and says:

"Silvia, come inside. We are going to Geneva now."

I look at Duck, anxious: "Go on! Tell me!"

"Last night," Duck says, "he comes home very late and doesn't want to wake up grandma. Because she would've kept nagging him *why did you drink again* and so on. And he's hungry, right? So he looks for some food in the kitchen. He looks in this pot and that pot and finds some soup in one of them. So he starts eating it. And this morning I hear him telling grandma:

'Ileana, you should've boiled that meat in the red pot a little bit more, Ileana, I couldn't eat a morsel of it, it was that hard to chew!'

And grandma says:

'You fool, you drank again last night, didn't you?'

'Who, me? Drank?' says grandpa and crosses himself. 'So help me God if I drank.'

'So help you God, ha?' says grandma. 'The devil will take charge of your soul as soon as you die, not a second later, because you take God's name in vain on a holy Sunday! So you see, you old fool, how drunk you were, in the red pot I had a dishcloth with which I cleaned the pot, on top of which I added some water and let it there till morning. That water was for the pig slops and that thing you chewed on was the dishcloth, not a piece of meat!'"

"He tried to eat the dishcloth?!" I ask, and Duck nods to me, shaken with laughter. We both laugh so hard that our eyes fill with tears. We stop to breathe for a second, and then break again into cascades of laughter.

That is when my father opens the door and says again:

"Come on, didn't you hear what I said? We're leaving, come on! You have plenty of time to laugh when school starts, come on now!"

I look at Duck and shrug my shoulders. What can I do?

"Oh, don't worry," Duck says, go on. "I'll tell you the rest tomorrow!"

We stand up and say goodbye. But after a few steps we turn and burst into laughter again as Duck, stopped at the gate, mimics her grandfather dutifully chewing the dishcloth.

I go inside, still laughing, but I stop soon because father's face is somber.

"Why are we going to Geneva?" I ask.

"His house," father explains, "was vandalized by thieves last night. He just called Aneta and told her to let us know. It's a pity your mother is working and cannot come with us, but at least the three of us can go. We can see if he needs any help."

Geneva is my uncle. His real name is Vasile, not Geneva, but no one calls him that. I know why, because my father told me the whole story many times. When Vasile was younger, he kept saying that he wanted to go and visit, out of all the cities in the world, the Swiss town of Geneva. He had heard about the Geneva Convention and had a few questions, he said, regarding his human rights. He figured that someone in that city might help him with that. As soon as he had the money, he made an application for a passport. His application was immediately rejected, of course, without any explanation.

That, however, didn't stop him. For about five years, twice a year, he submitted a passport request, but since no authority could ever conceive why a peasant, out of the blue, would want to visit Geneva, they kept rejecting his application over and over. Everyone in his village who knew about it thought his stubbornness was quite comical and they started calling him Geneva instead of Vasile.   After a while, even the government workers in charge of rejecting his application said, every time he came up with a new one:

"Again, Geneva? Do you never tire, Geneva?"

And Geneva remained his name.

"Hurry up," says father, "we have to catch the 11 o'clock bus to Golesti. Mirela, are you ready?"

"I'm ready," says Mirela, with sleepy eyes.

We leave. It is a two bus trip, because Geneva lives out in the country, where he can raise his horses, cows, countless chickens, ducks and geese. To get there, we have to board bus number 3 first, that takes us to the outskirts of the city of Bacau. Except for a woman carrying a bag with five loaves of bread, we are the only people at the bus stop. Bus number 3 comes immediately and is not crowded, which is unusual for a Sunday morning. We even have seats. As soon as we get in, the bus driver starts the bus, quite suddenly, so Mirela has trouble standing. She instinctively stretches her hand in front of her to grab something, but the bar close to her runs out of her grasp, with the bus's first jerk. Father supports both of us with his right hand, so we don't fall. In the next second, we are both seated, rather forcefully, by the next jerk of the old bus.

"A little gentleness wouldn't hurt!" my father says, loudly, so the driver can hear him.

"You are not transporting potatoes here, you know, Mr. Driver!" says an old lady who sits two rows further back. "He did the same thing when we boarded," she continues toward my father. "He does it on purpose! He doesn't care!"

"Why should he care?" the woman who boarded with us says. "If he drives well, he 's paid. If he drives badly, he's paid."

"He's un-touchable!" a man in the back laughs.

The old lady turns toward him and says:

"Some people just talk to hear their voices!"

The man doesn't respond, and after a few seconds starts whistling softly. From where I sit, I see half of the driver's face in the mirror. He has a dark face with very black hair and dark big eyes. He seems pretty young. He doesn't appear to hear what his passengers say about him. He just drives, his eyes fixed on the street ahead of him.

In 15 minutes, we are out of this bus and wait for the second one, bus number 5, that only comes once every hour. In and around the bus stop, there is already a sea of people waiting. Most of them are peasants, going back to their houses with bags and knapsacks filled with everything one can imagine, from wool to shoes to beans to bread. Those knapsacks, together with the throng of owners, must get into a bus that probably doesn't have more than thirty seats.

"Be careful now," father says. "When the bus comes, try to get close to the middle door, do you understand? And follow me!"

He holds our hands. In a few minutes, the empty bus arrives. As we come closer to the crowd, we do our best to position ourselves toward the middle of the bus, moving along the bus and trying to guess where it will stop. After puffing and huffing, the bus stops and opens its doors with a squeaky jerk. I find myself propelled by a huge force onto the first stair of the bus, then the second. I don't know where Mirela and my father are, and I have no time to look for them. I respond instinctively to the brute force that swarms around me. I don't move fast enough. Seconds cost me seats: too late for this one, too late for that one onto which a man throws his knapsack from a distance, to reserve it. Then an old lady literally pushes me away when I am almost ready to get the third one. Among all these fat, big women with chintzy skirts, red faces and huge breasts, I don't stand a chance. I am happy when I am pushed into a skinny space between the driver's cabin and the first seat of the bus, on which the woman who pushed me aside sits holding a basket with something moving inside, perhaps live chicks. I look around me and I see father sitting, with Mirela on his lap, in the third row.

"Come on here" he says, pointing toward a little space on his other knee. "Come here."

But things are not settled inside the bus. People still try to board, although there is no space to throw a pin, as someone points out.

"There is no more space, madam," says a boy hanging by the bars attached to bus's front door. "Stop pushing me," he says to a woman who wears a red silk scarf on her head, "don't you see there is no more space?"

"Please try a little bit more, for one more person," that woman responds, trying to get a grasp of the bar. "Just a little, why is that so difficult?"

"Don't you see there is no more space inside?" says someone. "Wait for the 12 o'clock one!"

"Oh yes? You wouldn't talk like that, giving all kind of smart advice if you were in my place!" responds the woman with red scarf.

"But the thing is, I'm not!" the response comes quickly. "See? That's the difference between us! I'm in and you're out!"

People laugh. The woman with the silk scarf lets go, and takes a few steps away, moving her lips slowly as she carries her backpack toward the shade of a tree. After a few unsuccessful attempts to close the door, each time accompanied by screams and yells (*"Oh, no, don't close the damn door now!"* *"My elbow!"* *"Au! Are you trying to kill us, driver?"*) the driver gives up and starts the bus as it is, with people hanging dangerously out of the doors. There is no way I could move from where I am. I look toward father, and he sees that as well. He raises his hand and says "You're fine there, stay there!" I feel privileged to have my little corner with only one side toward humans. In that little niche, I travel securely for the next one and a half hours. And during that time, a person, maybe two, gets off the bus, only to have five people trying desperately to board the bus at each stop.

I am happy when I'm out. Having no elbows pounding in my ribcage feels luxurious. As we start walking toward Geneva's house, father says, rather to himself:

"It's always crowded on Sundays. But what can you do?"

We stop for a second. Mirela arranges her beautiful white dress, I pull up the sleeves of my green blouse. Father runs his hand through the little hair left on his head. I feel the sun burning the top of my head.

"I'm hot," I say to my father.

"Daddy, I'm hot, too," says Mirela.

"We'll be there in no time, you'll see," says my father.

But I know that's a bit of an overstatement. We still have to walk at least forty minutes on a country road, among big trees and wild bushes. The road is not paved, and thus it is full of holes, stones and patches of grass, although as soon as we get in the shade it's not so bad.

"Isn't this nice?" says my father, walking fast, with his big steps.

Mirela and I try to keep up, and run ahead of him from time to time, so we can then slow down for a few seconds and catch our breath waiting for him. After a while, the village appears in front of us, with its little church up on the hill, white houses, fenced yards, the smell of smoke and countless noises made by all kinds of animals, big and small.

Geneva's house is somewhat different from those around it. It is bigger, has a larger yard and has a remarkable amount of junk all around, such as an abandoned tractor, a rusty combine that never worked and some old machinery for processing flour that now processes droppings of some winged resident. Every time we come here my cousins take me around to show me their dad's latest acquisition in this museum of failed technology. Now, Geneva is in front of his house, where he has his herb garden. He also has a larger garden toward the back of his house, where he grows corn, beans, and clover. But the land where all the serious growing takes place is way far behind the hills on which the village is situated. That is land that once belonged to the villagers - each with his own patch, larger or smaller, passed down from generation to generation. Now, after collectivization, all that land belongs to all and none, my father says. Even worse, most products obtained from that collectivized land go to the state. Only a small portion can be kept by the peasants, according to some devilish, as I heard aunt Aneta call it, quota.

When he sees us coming, Geneva, bent to pick something from the garden, straightens up and greets us.

"Good afternoon, Vasile" says my father, as we open the gate.

"Good afternoon, good afternoon," says Geneva. He comes close to us, shakes father's hand and pats Mirela and me on our heads.

"Come in, come in…"

We all go onto the patio that is also an open air kitchen where the family cooks and eats during summer and early fall. There is a stove, a table and a kitchen counter with some shelves above it.

"Have a seat," says Geneva. "I need some newspaper…"

He looks around, and finds some on one of the higher shelves above the stove. He shakes the pages open, and places the bunch of onions he just picked on it. The onions fall in relative disarray, and cover the fine print of the newspaper. It is *Scinteia*, the official governmental newspaper. Between the soiled roots of the onions I can read: *Socialism victoriously conquers Romanian villages...*

"So tell me more about your troubles," says father. "How did it happen?"

"So last night, we went to bed at 10 o'clock. I said my prayer, made a round in the stables...and came back. The three month old calf had been languid all day long...I went to see how he was. After I fell asleep, I heard some noises...I don't know what time it was...I thought I was dreaming. I should have woken up..."

"Well, better you didn't...who knows what those criminals were up to...they kill you for nothing..."

"Of, of, of," Geneva sighs. "I wrote a letter to the police and I made a list of things they stole."

He gets up and slowly goes inside the house. My sister starts moaning.

"Daddy, I wanna go and see the calf..."

"You'll see the animals later."

"No, now!"

"Stay still," father says. "Do you want to get dung all over your white dress?"

Mirela considers. No, you can clearly see she doesn't want anything on her white dress. She says nothing, and just purses her lips into a little rabbit mouth.

Geneva is back, with a piece of paper filled with tight handwriting on one side. He gives it to my father. From where I am, I can see very well what's written on that piece of paper, and along with my father, who looks carefully at it, I read it with interest. It is a letter that Geneva wrote in longhand, in his terrible handwriting. I can barely decipher it but as I read it, I can see it becomes more and more interesting:

"Vasile Cojea from Golesti, county of Bacau, declare that during the night of August 19, 1968, the following were stolen from me by thieves and criminals:

10 jars of tomato paste

1 bale of lamb's wool

1 sickle

10,000 lei

2 green and black blankets

I am appealing to you to help me find the thieves and criminals that vandalized my house so I can get back the goods I worked hard to acquire with the sweat of my forehead.

Respectfully yours,

Vasile Geneva Cojea"

Father puts down the letter and looks at Geneva.

"Did you send this to the police already?"

"Not yet," says Geneva.

"Good," says father. "You have here the essentials, but you need to write up a more official letter, you know?"

"Scurtu doesn't want a letter, all he wants is a bribe. He couldn't care less about letters."

"Well," says father. "Even so, you have to let them know in an official way what happened. And you have to be a bit careful here. When you write this letter, you have to address it properly. For example: state your name, address, ID card number and so on. Then, describe the situation: tell them when you think your house was broken into, if you heard anything, and if you suspect anyone."

Geneva follows father with interest.

"And then," father continues, pointing toward the middle of the page, "when you list the items they stole from you, Vasile, start with the most important ones. Start with 10,000 lei, not with tomato paste jars, understand? That is a lot of money and that's what they should try to find first! Let's write it again! Do you have some paper and a pen?"

"I'll bring it, just a moment," says Geneva, and goes back inside the house.

"Can we go now and see the animals?" says Mirela, stretching. "I want to see the calf!"

"Stay still," father responds. "You'll see him soon, he's not going anywhere! He's waiting patiently for you!"

"Really?" Mirela says. "He knows?"

"Oh yes. That's a very smart calf. Just stay still and when your cousins come back you'll go with them to play and see all the animals." He doesn't even finish his sentence when the gate opens and my aunt Eugenia with my two cousins, Mihai and Ilie, enter the yard. They are all dressed up in their best clothes. Eugenia wears a black skirt and blouse, and black shoes with low heels and the two boys wear black pants and white shirts. They all have the pious air of people who just escaped sacred containment and are happy to be back to the accidents of life, to its irregularities. Speaking of which: as they come close to us, Mihai stumbles over a stone and almost falls. He manages to keep his equilibrium by beating the air with his hands. He recovers, and lets a "What the hell!" out of his mouth in full force. His mother smacks him on his head immediately:

"Not even fifteen minutes passed since you left the House of God! Today is the holy Sunday!"

That embarrasses him even more and he looks at his mother reproachfully.

They are now by the table, and we cousins hug and kiss on the cheeks.

"Welcome, Dan," says Eugenia to my father, hugging him.

"It's good to see you," says father. "Geneva told me this morning about the troubles you are having. Who do you think broke into your house?"

"It must be," she says, pulling a chair and sitting at the table with us, "it must be the Plum brothers. Those vagabonds never worked and never did anything good with their lives since they came to live in this village with their grandmother. I'm pretty sure it's the Plums. All their family was like that: a bunch of thieves and losers! A shame for this village!"

She stops for a second then whispers in a pained tone:

"Ten thousand lei, Dan!"

She has tears in her eyes.

"Be trustful that they'll find the thieves!" father says to his sister. "Don't lose hope!"

"I don't know! I spoke with Scurtu - you know Scurtu, don't you? The new policeman here in Golesti. I told him. He says: write a petition and give that to me. I'll take care of you! I have children to send to school too! So," Eugenia continues, "what is he telling me, not by his words but by the way he looks at me? I'll tell you what he's telling me: bribe me, that's what he's telling me!"

"Maybe he didn't mean that, now!"

"Oh, yes, you'll see! I bet not ten thousand, but twenty-five thousand lei that he'll be here as soon as he gets home from church and put his policeman's uniform on! He can not let this opportunity go by."

"Oh, you're seeing everything too dark!"

Geneva pours everyone a glass of plum brandy, then takes a piece of paper and starts writing. He frowns at the paper, concentrating hard.

Eugenia stands up.

"I'd better go and prepare some lunch!"

One of the reasons I don't like to come here too often (besides the bus ride) is the food. It's not the taste. The food is always tasty - especially because we have to work so hard to get here from the city that by the time we're eating, we're tired like mules. The real reason I don't like food is almost every time we eat here I find some kind of insect in it. Last time it was half a fly. Not even the skinny grey one, but that fat green long-winged kind that bites horses and cows. And the way it looked in my soup, faded in color as vegetables are after long boiling, I deduced that it had entered the soup at an early stage in its preparation.

My cousins come out of the house after changing their clothes. They don't get out of the house one by one, like you'd expect human beings to do. Instead, they fight each other, pushing and shoving in the narrow space of the doorway and then burst out as if some brake inside their bodies has been released. They both yell, happy, I suppose, to have guests.

"Want to see the animals?" says Ilie, the youngest, as he is approaching us.

"Yes, I want to," says Mirela. "I'm coming!"

"Bring some eggs back, Ilie," says his mother, who has placed about four big pots on the stove.

She starts the fire in the wood stove and I feel the smoke when the breeze blows it toward us.

"Feed the pig, here!" she says to her older son, pouring some kind of liquid into a bigger pot that always hangs on the fence nearby. The liquid contains lumps of food, all falling with slurping noises into pig's red pot.

"Take it, here," Eugenia says.

Each of the boys takes a handle of the pot, which is not too big but probably heavy and start carrying it toward the back of the house. Mirela is all excited, and follows the procession, jumping up and down.

"Such a pity for her white dress," says Eugenia. "Dan, you should've had her wear something else if she wanted to play with the calf!"

"Don't get dirty!" says my father.

Then to me:

"What are you doing, aren't you going? Go and take care of Mirela!"

"I don't want to go!"

171

"Go and play! See the calf! Go with them!"

"No!"

"Why not?"

"Because I want to stay here with you."

"Don't you want to see the animals?"

"I want to see Scurtu," I respond.

"Go," says my father, "and take care of Mirela if you don't want to see animals. Go and take care of your sister!"

I really don't want to go. I want to stay here at this table with Geneva and my father and Eugenia nearby to hear what they say about the thieves. This is far more interesting than a pig and a calf. But in order to be able to stay, I know I have to earn it. I have to make a strong enough argument to persuade my father.

"I don't want to go and see a calf," I say to my father, "just because Mirela does. What am I, her guardian angel?"

Geneva snorts. Father looks at me, amused:

"This one, where did you hear this one, now?"

I shrug.

"Let her alone," says Eugenia. "If she doesn't want to go, she doesn't want to go."

I am relieved. And in the next second happy, because the gate opens and the new policeman, Scurtu, appears. He wears his official hat and his policeman's uniform. I look at Eugenia and Eugenia looks at my father with a "...told you so!" expression on her face.

"Good afternoon," says Scurtu.

"Good afternoon," says Eugenia.

Scurtu and my father shake hands.

"Have a seat, Mr. Scurtu."

Geneva stands up, goes in the kitchen and comes back with a glass for Scurtu. He pours plum brandy for dad, Scurtu and Eugenia, and then they lift their glasses.

"Cheers!" says Scurtu. "May you be in good health!"

Everyone agrees, and drinks at once. I watch how they all, as if hit by some spell, throw their head back and swallow that drink at once.

"Uaaaa! Good stuff!" says Scurtu. "Good stuff!"

My father places his glass on the table and says:

"So I understand you'll start an investigation, right away, is that true?"

"Yes, yes, an investigation," says Scurtu, nodding approvingly as Geneva pours him another glass.

"We have the petition here," says father, pointing to the new petition that Geneva has just finished writing.

"You can take it," says Geneva, "here you are!"

"No, no, no," says Scurtu. "Hold on to it! I can't take it now!"

"Why not?" asks Eugenia, turning toward us as she pours some more corn flour in polenta.

"Because," Scurtu responds, "this is an official document and I cannot take it home. But I can talk about it. Actually, that's what I came for," says Scurtu, "to talk with Genevá for a few minutes."

Geneva stands up and says:

"Come inside the house, Mr. Scurtu, come in."

Both men go inside the house. Eugenia puts down the spoon she was using to mix the polenta and looks at my father. She whispers:

"I told you...this Scurtu...He's going to ask for money! You'll see! That leech!"

She stays still, but her expression is angry. I can see she's torn by opposite wishes: she'd like to go inside (by the way she looks around and toward the house) but something prevents her from moving, keeping her there in front of her four boiling pots. She sighs, and resumes stirring.

Geneva and Scurtu come out of the house, and Scurtu takes his hat off, passes his hand through his hair, puts the hat back on and says to everyone:

"I'd better get going! Do my inspection rounds! Good bye, now!"

Then toward Geneva:

"Bring that petition at 8 o'clock sharp tomorrow morning to the police station! Yes?"

"Yes, yes," says Geneva.

After Scurtu leaves and is out of sight, Eugenia turns toward Geneva:

"You gave him money, didn't you?"

Geneva pours one round of plum brandy for himself and father and says: "He asked for money! I gave him fifty lei, otherwise he would not even start an investigation!"

"So if he asked you for money, you had to give him money? Just like that?"

"Oh, come on, let it be! We need him to help us! Don't make such a big fuss!"

"A fuss?" says Eugenia. "This is fuss? You'll see fuss when he come back tomorrow for money again! This man is not the one to put people in jail. He's the one who should go to jail and lock the gates after himself for life!"

She stirs the polenta with quick moves and shakes her head.

"And," she continues after a few seconds, "he's making a round of inspection, ha? I tell you what his inspection is! Collecting all kinds of bribes from people! I bet you he's going now to the Plums to collect his bribe from them too. And this is how he fills his pockets. And then, we'll never find out who stole our goods. This is what is going to happen," she says, taking the polenta pot from the stove and placing it on a big plate.

The polenta is large, bright yellow, and enveloped in clouds of steam that raise straight up a few centimeters before they dissolve in the hot air of the afternoon.

"Better get those kids back," she says to Geneva, "and have them wash their hands. Lunch is ready!"

My cousins and my sister appear, each running to be the first one to sit at the table.

"Go and wash your hands, go!" Eugenia says to them.

All three at once rush toward the bucket of water. Close by, there are a bunch of mugs hanging from nails on the wall. Mihai takes a mug, fills it with water and pours for his brother and Mirela. They all rub their palms briskly under the thin stream of water, then shake them dry. When his turn comes, the youngest son Ilie pretends to do the same, but saves some water in his palms and sprinkles everyone around him. A large chorus of hi hi hi and ha ha ha erupts. Mihai smacks him.

"Enough now! Everyone at the table!" Eugenia says.

"How was it," I ask Mirela. "Did you see the calf?"

177

"He's big! And he has big beautiful eyes!" Mirela replies, elated. "Daddy, can we have a calf?"

"Sure," father responds. "A plastic one."

Our cousins laugh.

"Not a plastic one!" cries Mirela. "A real one!"

"Where are you going to raise him? In bed with you?" laughs Mihai.

"Noooo!" says Mirela, her face all red.

Eugenia brings the polenta and the fried chicken. Then fried potatoes and a tomato salad.

We eat, sometimes blowing on little pieces of polenta which are still hot but gluey and tasty.

"If you come back next week, we'll have little chicks," says Ilie to Mirela. "Have you ever seen them hatching?"

"Daddy, can we come next week? Can we?"

"Next week," father says, "you are going to stay with your grandmother while Silvia is at the camp."

"You're going to the camp?" asks Ilie.

I nod, my mouth full of polenta. My cousins look enviously at me.

"At the Black sea," I finally respond. "I can't wait!"

"She already packed as if she goes to Patagonia," my father says. "Two full suitcases."

"Good for her," Eugenia says. "She deserves it, because she has such good marks in school. You should follow her example," Eugenia says, looking toward her sons.

They look down at their plates, then slowly raise their eyes and throw a mischievous look at me. I do the same, and when our eyes meet, we all three burst into laughter.

"Don't praise her too much," father says. "If she could, she would go to a school where all you have to do is lie in bed and read stories about flying horses. When she grows up, she'll look up in the sky and be disappointed that she's not seeing any!"

"But at least she reads," Eugenia says. "I know some people who run around all day long doing nothing!"

I think at what she's saying and although I have not been in their house for more than a couple of days in a row, I know how hard the life of these children is. I know they wake up at five o'clock to till corn, harvest wheat, or pull weeds for weeks and weeks during summer. I know they prepare food for the animals too, take the cows to pasture, and stay there with them all day long. I know they never go to see a movie, like we sometimes do. They have, besides their schoolbooks, which are free, only two books in the whole house: one Almanac from 1934 and a book about a shepherd who lived with his sheep on the top of a mountain until he became a saint. I know that my cousins believe my family is better off, because they often tell me that they would like to live in the city where there are cars, and streets, and shops, and packed butter, and noise.

"How long are you going to stay at the seaside?" Ilie asks.

"Two weeks. We first go to Constanta, where we stop and visit the Danube harbor, and then we go to the Black Sea beach, and stay there the rest of the time."

"Do you swim?"

I look at my father and say, cautiously:

"No, I am not going to swim."

"What's the fun of going to the seaside if you don't swim," says Geneva.

I try to change the subject.

"I haven't seen any bees," I say to Mihai.

"Oh, they died," says Mihai.

My father stops eating.

"How's that?"

"Listen to this now," Eugenia intervenes. "Some...people...from the County's Agricultural Department came...with a small plane and sprayed over the village with pesticides... and killed all the bees...Not even one bee survived. No one has bees around here anymore."

Father shakes his head.

"Such idiots," he says. "How can you spray like an idiot without knowing what you are doing? Did they compensate you?"

"Not even one leu," responds Eugenia. "Not even one leu."

We eat in silence. Around us, the heat has mellowed a bit, and a faint breeze twists a leaf here and there. On the dusty road in front of Geneva's house, solitary figures pass slowly, a child or a woman, all dressed up in Sunday clothes. The day is almost gone – less than half of it remains. That half will pass quickly as we'll probably leave soon, to complete our adventures in the unpredictable world of bus traveling.

And that leaves less than one week until camp.

The country is burning, and missus ...

It is morning. The morning of August 22nd. Only two more days to camp! I am on vacation, and so I don't have to wake up - I can laze in bed as long as my heart desires. But then, as I turn and cuddle near Mirela, I hear sounds in the room. The sound of clinked silverware. Someone stirring liquid in a cup. The smell of coffee. The sounds of the morning, almost always accompanied by whispers, my mom saying to my father *We have to do this and we have to do that, we have to purchase this and that,* and my father's voice, *Again? We spend money again? Go and spend all the money, go, go,* my father whispers, and mom saying *Don't you see we need it,* and father responding *All I see is that you want to spend money again,* all those morning discussions - or, like last week, my father saying *The girls should go to the countryside for a*

183

few weeks now, maybe it would be better to send them there, you never know what happens... Yes, it's a good idea, mom agrees, well, all those discussions are not taking place today. Not today.

Today, my mother and my father sit silently at the kitchen table, quite close to the bed where Mirela and I sleep. I see them both from profile. They sit quiet and motionless looking at the cup of coffee in front of them. For minutes now, neither of them says a word. I open my eyes more and look at them again, carefully. Maybe they had a fight, and now they won't talk to each other. But then my mom stands up, gets the pot of coffee and pours some more in my father's cup. Then, they return to watching the air above their coffee cups. Now *that* I have not seen before. I raise my head a little bit, and watch them warily. My father, I can see now, has tears in his eyes. He looks at me without saying anything, then he turns his eyes away and looks again at the mysterious point above his coffee cup. My next thought is: he must have had a little glass of plum brandy early in the morning. When he drinks, my father becomes emotional and many times recites from his favorite Romanian writers, such as Delavrancea. In particular, he makes a wonderful Stephan the Great. As he recites, he holds his glass up in the air, as if it is a bird ready to take off, and he has tears in his eyes. I quickly look at my mother: if he's *abtiguit* (that is, slightly tipsy, neither drunk nor sober) she will look in a certain way to me and I'll know.

But now my mother's eyes are serious and somber, and she doesn't even seem to notice me. Finally I can not take it anymore. I raise my head from the pillow and ask him:

"Dad? Why are you crying?"

My father looks at me: "Your daddy is going to war, Silvia."

And then he turns his eyes away from me, toward that invisible target that seems to absorb all his attention.

"The Russians have invaded Czechoslovakia," my mother says. "War may be coming our way."

Now I start to understand how unusual this actually is, because as I fully wake up, I see that it is almost nine o'clock. My father always leaves for work at six.

"And you're not going to work anymore, if it's war?"

And then it suddenly comes to me: stuuuupid question, Silvia! If it is war, it's war! Nothing else

185

happens when it's war. Everything stops for the war. No work, no school. No summer camp.

"There's going to be no summer camp, right," I articulate slowly, looking at my mother, pronouncing each word carefully as if the mere act of enouncing it might render it fatally real.

"Right?" I ask again, on the same flat tone.

My mother and father look at me. Now my mother also has tears in her eyes:

"Silvia dear, I know how much you wanted to go, dear, but there is nothing anyone can do."

My head is empty. Crystal clear empty. Peace. Silence. An immense, solid silence, the one after the lightning and before the thunder. And then, in a gust I cannot control, understand or stop, tears come over me like the flood of the century, abolishing my mind and my will, taking me away and dissolving me into it, and then carrying me far, far away, into the Lands of Weeping and Despair where there is nothing: no hope, no life, nothing, nothing, nothing, just the feeling of utter, total, incomprehensible rage and despair, the most unbelievable sorrow that everything is lost, and nothing, nothing will ever matter again. I cry with long sobs that shake the bed. My sister wakes up and looks at me with her large, beautiful dark eyes.

"Oh, my dear, don't cry," says my mother, coming by my side of the bed and hugging me with her soft arms. "Don't cry so hard. You'll go next year!"

An hour later, I sit on the bench in front of my house. My mind is still empty. I am by now resigned to the idea that everything is lost, although deep down in my heart, against my better judgment, I still secretly hope the camp will still start, maybe one week later.

"Don't you understand," my mother told me, "don't you understand what a war is? You are almost 11 years old by now. I shouldn't have to explain everything to you like I have to do with Mirela." My mother sometimes talks with me as if I am the grown-up, and I guess I am the grown-up, compared to Mirela. But I am - like she said with her own mouth - only 10 years old. "You cry your heart out that you cannot go to a summer camp. But don't you see that the world is going topsy-turvy? *Tara arde si baba se piaptana.* You'd better stop that lamentation and do something good with your time. Better go and buy some bors so I can finish up our lunch for today."

"I don't want to get any bors!" I say and I get out of the house. Then, not knowing what to do next, I look around in all directions and I decide to sit on the bench by the old pear. "Tara arde si baba se piaptana" means "The country is burning and missus is combing her hair." Is the country burning? I look around. Nothing is happening. All I see is an empty yard, with a brown fence around it, and our house still covered by the shadows of the morning. Plus a pale blue sky above. But maybe outside our yard, on the streets, something *is* *happening*. Perhaps I should take a look. So a few minutes later I go back inside.

"I am going to get bors," I say.

My mother comes and caresses my hair.

"Do you think I do not understand how disappointed you are, my dear? But now we are going through hard times. The whole country is. You have to learn to deal with it."

"Mom, are there going to be fights on the streets? On our street?"

"Who knows," mom says. "Your father just left for a meeting with all the people in his plant. We'll just have to wait and see. But I think and hope it's going to be fine, she says, holding me in her arms and caressing my head. It's going to be fine."

A few moments later she gives me one leu and points toward the shelves where the bors bottles are.

"Why don't you take Mirela with you," she says.

I might as well. I open the cupboard, take the two empty milk bottles and put them in the raffia bag. Mirela is outside. I call her in.

"I'm not coming," she responds, poking with a stick in the grass, "I don't wanna go."

"You can wear my crown!" I say. "All the way to the Lecca sisters and back!"

Her eyes open up.

"I can?"

"Sure you can. The beautiful yellow crown."

At the last crafts lesson of the year, we each made something from flexible cardboard. We could make a cube, or a cylinder, or a little house. I chose to make a crown. It turned out to be quite a gorgeous one after I covered it with the yellow tinfoil aunt Aneta gave me. I liked it so much that I wore it for a few weeks - to the envy of my sister - every time I went out to play.

Mirela comes, takes the crown and puts it on her head. It is a bit large, but not too much. Her pretty little blond head looks good in it, although her ears stick out a bit. She is happy.

"You are very pretty," mom says to her.

Mirela's eyes glow with joy.

I grab the raffia bag with the bottles, take Mirela's hand and go out. As we open the door, Mirela stops.

"I don't want to come with you anymore."

"But you promised! I gave you my crown! Now you must do what I ask you to do."

She looks at me with her beautiful dark eyes.

"Don't you see *I am* the queen now?"

Oh sure. How did I forget?

"All right," I say, "what does Your Majesty want now?"

"I want you," Mirela says seriously, "to draw a house for me when we come back. A tiny house."

Oh, well, I think. I might as well do whatever she wants. What else am I going to do anyway till school starts.

"All right, a tiny house," I agree. "You've got it."

We walk in silence on the curb, hand in hand. Near me, Mirela steps importantly, holding her crowned head with glory and dignity. We stop at each intersection, look carefully left and right, then cross the street. We don't meet one single person on the street although it's almost 11 in the morning, an hour when usually the streets swarm with people.

"There's no one on the street," I say to Mirela. "See?"

"Yes. But you have to talk to me like you talk to a queen, remember?" she says, suddenly stopping.

"Oh, I'm sorry, Your Majesty. And do you know why, Your Highness, there is no one on the streets?" I ask her.

"No, why?"

"Because it's war, Your Highness," I respond, in a low voice.

"How do you know?"

"Mom and Dad told me."

"That's why you cried this morning?"

I think about it. Was it? Yes, maybe.

"Yes, that's why I cried," I respond.

She nods, and, stopping for a second, takes her hand from my hand and adjusts her crown.

"You look wonderful, Your Majesty!" I say.

She looks at me, amused and dignified at the same time.

We are in front of the enemy's house. His yard is empty and the house seems deserted. No movement of any kind. Blinds cover every window. The same goes for almost every house we pass by.

I ring at Ana and Crina's door. Crina opens the door just a crack, barely enough for me to see her face. She doesn't smile.

"Good morning," I say. "Mom would like two liters of bors."

"Come in dear, come in, don't stay there!"

We step in, and say good morning again. Ana and Mr. Gogu, their neighbor, are in the room as well. They greet us briefly, then go back to their conversation. Crina takes my bag and starts filling the first bottle. After the first bottle is full, she stops and caresses Mirela's cheek:

"Aren't you a pretty queen, my dear! What queen are you?"

"I'm the Queen of Dawn," Mirela responds, proudly.

Mr. Gogu turns to her, looks for a second at us and says: "And these children. Just starting their lives now. At least we lives a little until the red pest came and took over our lives."

"Only God knows what's going to happen!" Ana says, touching her chin with her right hand. "Only God knows."

"I remember it was 1953," Mr. Gogu says. "My nephew and I were in a restaurant. That morning they had announced on radio that Stalin died. And a man at a table nearby, a common acquaintance who had had one too many drinks, Gelu was his name, raised a glass of plum brandy and said to everyone around him, 'May God rest Comrade Stalin's soul in peace!'

And do you know what happened? Two men from another table stood up, came to this friend of ours and said, 'You, come with us!' A week later I met Gelu's wife. Crying on the street, poor woman. First I thought she had lost her minds. Her husband had been arrested and sent to jail just like that. Seven years of jail, this is what he got, she said, for saying God rest Stalin's soul. Five months later Gelu died in jail. He was an old man. You don't send an old man to jail for some words he said while drinking. I tell you, if these red pests come over us again, we may as well kill ourselves before their tanks cross our borders...The evil, I tell you, the evil is still to come...That's why all communists should be shot, one by one...and someone should start right from the top..."

"They will not invade us," Crina says, rinsing the ladle. "They are too busy with the Czechs."

"Who knows," Mr Gogu says. "Our country is in a state of heightened alert. Anything can happen."

"It's true," Ana says.

Then pointing toward us, Ana continues:

"Maybe we should not scare the children! I saw you've got some wonderful Splendor roses, Mr. Gogu!"

Mr. Gogu turns toward Ana, and doesn't say anything for a few seconds. Than he pronounces, slowly:

"They'll see worse times than these when they grow up. This is only the tip of the iceberg. At least they'll remember our words and they'll understand why it will be getting worse and worse. Isn't that true, Silvia?"

I look at him. He is an old man I rarely see, but somehow I have the feeling I've known him for ages. I understand that he, Mr. Gogu, is the one who, with his warnings, adds clarity to this fuzzy knowledge that swarms around me. He is the only one who does not try to shield me, like my parents do, from what's happening around us. I feel that my duty is to pay attention, so that someday - one day, one lifetime later, sometime - I will be able to remember his words. Our deal is thus simple and complicated at the same time, and I am definitely going to keep my end of it. That's for sure. So right now I just look into his eyes and nod.

"It's one leu, dear," Crina says, and gives me the bag with bors bottles.

I give her the money and take Mirela's hand. We say goodbye. Crina closes the door behind us, and we walk back home, slowly crossing the empty streets after we carefully look left and right. From time to time, I slightly raise the bag to reposition the handles in my hand. I do that as gently as I can. The bottles knock one each other slightly when I raise the bag. Mirela stops for a second and waits for my left hand, and uses that second to better arrange her crown. She is wearing it with dignity and charm. She tells me, a bit sad, that it's a pity it's war.

"Why," I ask.

"Because otherwise there would be people on the streets and they could admire my beautiful yellow crown," she says.

I arrive home and give my mom the bors bottles, then I go outside in the yard. I sit on the bench where my father smacked me because I said 7 times 6 is 41. Three long weeks of vacation stare back at me. I have no idea what can I do besides reading and then reading some more. Duck is at her grandparents, all my other friends are away. For the first time, I feel that the real life has become as strange as the tales I read. Empty streets. People not smiling anymore. And the worse is to come, as Mr. Gogu said. A new tale - an evil one – must have jumped out of some book and has taken over the world. So I am pleased when I see the Queen of

Dawn (who's been probing the ground with a stick all over the yard) coming toward me with a drawing pad and colored pencils.

"Come on, you promised! Please, draw me a house, only a house!"

She sits on the bench toward my right.

So I draw a house (straight walls, the roof, a window behind which you can see the face of a child) and I add - out of the kindness of my heart - three trees, a fence and a gate with king-size handles.

"Now, you have to put some curtains at the window," my sister says. "And add some pots of flowers in front of the fence."

I draw curtains and pots and when I'm done, I also plant a chimney on the roof. Heavy smoke coils out of it and an incandescent lemon yellow sun shines down on everything.

I give her the pad back.

"And the children? Where are the children who play in the yard?"

I draw two children, then a dog and a lamb, always difficult to tell apart, so I explain to her, pointing toward each animal:

"See? I made you a dog and a lamb."

Mirela is thrilled for a few seconds. Then a cloud appears on her face:

"And the sleigh? Where's the sleigh?"

"Which sleigh? Don't you see it's sunny outside? It's summer!"

"Oh yes? Then why is there smoke in the chimney and why aren't there any leaves in the trees? And no flowers around?"

I draw leaves. I draw flowers. I draw a sleigh.

"Now," my sister adds, pointing toward the left corner of the house, "make some big pebbles here. Big pebbles where a child falls over and gets his neck broken!"

"Gets his neck broken? What do you mean? Why would a child get his neck broken?"

"So you can," Mirela says, in a voice sweet as honey, "so you can draw the ambulance, the doctor and the hospital and the nurses, and how the doctor bandages his head and neck, and how his mother brings him tea, and she says drink your tea, and the child doesn't, so his mother beats him and the father comes and asks her why do you beat the sick child, and how she goes home and cries, and then they both come home, the father and the son, and the father and mother make up, so that, in the very end," Mirela says almost breathlessly, "so you can make a portrait of the three of them, all happy and smiling, in front of the house you promised you would draw for me!"

I look at her.

"You've got some guts, you know!"

She smiles.

So I flip the page and on a blank sheet I draw a hospital, an ambulance and a doctor with an oversized stethoscope hanging around his neck. Red drops fall from the head of the child, and the doctor holds his hand toward the sick child the way saints do on the walls of the church in my grandmother's village. I add a woman with a cup of tea in her hands. Mirela is overjoyed. She takes the pad in her hands and looks at it, for long minutes. Then, unexpectedly, she kisses me on my cheek.

"Thank you, Silvia!"

I kiss her on her cheek too.

"You're welcome, Your Majesty!"

She takes the pad and runs inside, to show it to mom. Just before entering the door, she turns around and comes back to me.

"Silvia," she says smiling, "you forgot to make a door!" She flips the pages to the first drawing, the one with the little house. Indeed, there is no door. Just a window; and a child behind the window.

"This house," I say slowly, "has no door."

"What do you mean, it has no door? All houses have doors. It cannot be a house without a door."

"Yes it can," I say.

She frowns:

"There is a child inside. How is he going to get out?"

"He's not. He's trapped inside."

"I don't like this house!" she says, and with a short move, she pulls that sheet out and tears it into small pieces. She smacks the pad on the bench, near me. Then, turning around, she finds a short stick fallen from the old pear tree, checks its strengths and, satisfied with it, goes back to poke the grass in the yard, the crown shinning on the top of her head under the afternoon's bright sun.

A child is a child, after all...

It's almost noon by now, and I am still sitting on the bench under the old pear tree. I'm not really doing anything. I doze off with a book, named "Stories of the Sea", in my lap. This is the book I was planning to take with me on my camp trip. I hold it, closed, in my lap. I don't want to open it or read it. I just want to know it's there, a captive, in my lap. "Poor book," I say. "You'll never travel to the sea you know so many stories about."

"What are you doing here?" aunt Aneta asks. "Talking to yourself?"

"No, to the book," I respond.

"Is your mother home?"

"Sure. She's inside."

I point toward the door, like she doesn't know where I live. She does know, of course: this is her house and we are renting two rooms from her. We pay a lot of money for the rent, mother says, but then she also says that it's worth paying a bit extra, because this way we have family nearby to help us. For example, if she needs someone to babysit Mirela for an hour or two unexpectedly, my aunt Aneta is always there to help. Plus, it's nice to have an aunt nearby, especially one who likes you. Aunt Aneta likes me because, as she once told someone, "You can talk with Silvia like you do with a grown-up." She is also proud that I have good grades in school: she had a hard time with her two now grown-up sons who could never wake up in time for school in the morning. And if they got inside the classroom, they found it terribly difficult to sit still for fifty minutes without falling asleep or dying of boredom. Aneta has told me many times that I have a bright future ahead of me. "When you grow up," she once told me, "I'll help you get a very good job. I'll help you get a telephone operator job." That must've been because that year Aneta had her telephone installed in her house and perhaps was so impressed with this marvel of human technology that any profession that had anything to do with a telephone became instantly magical as well. I did not really want to become a telephone operator, but I did not tell her that, because she then told me that when I grow up she'll show me how to write from right to left, like Arabs do. Now *that* I thought was really something because no one else, not even our teacher, Mrs. Popescu, knew how to write that way. But then, every time I asked her to actually show me how to write like an Arab, she said she didn't have time. So I started to suspect that she had just said that to hear herself say something fancy and that actually she had no idea how to write from right to left.

"Come inside," says Aneta, "I made a cherry pie for you guys. Call your sister too, where is she?"

"Mirelaaaa!" I call.

Mirela appears from behind the berry bushes, with her crown firm on her head and her probing stick in her right hand.

"What?"

"Aunt Aneta brought us cherry pie."

"Aaa...I don't wanna. I found a worm, and I cut it in two with the stick and it still moves. Do you wanna see it?"

"Nooo! I don't! You'd better come inside and wash your hands."

Her royal distinction takes charge of the situation. She stands up straight and says, coldly:

"No, thank you!"

And holding her crowned head up, she goes back behind the bushes.

I follow Aneta, who's now inside, talking with mom, as they slice the pie and place each slice on one plate.

"Because if they beat him, he's done! He's eighty years old!"

"Who is?" I ask.

Mother turns and looks sternly at me.

"Don't you know it's not polite to interfere with grown-ups conversations? Sit here and eat," says mom.

We all eat in silence. The pie is really good. The dough is crunchy and the layer of cherries, on top, is sweet and mellow and has just a hint of sourness.

"When did they take him?" asks mom.

"Half an hour ago," responds Aneta. "Mrs. Lazar told me. They planted a guy with blue eyes by his house all night long. Who knows why."

I know about those guys. Those blue eyed guys are some kind of policemen who watch people's houses. People call them "trees with ties," because they just stand by a person's house for hours and do nothing. And they wear suits and ties and have their hair cut really short.

"He was tending to his roses," Aneta continues, "when they came and took him. He just got some Splendor ones. Beautiful flowers, and they smell like a dream..."

"He must've done something," mom says, "they wouldn't take him away for nothing..."

Suddenly it's clear to me: they took Mr. Gogu to the Police!

"I know why!" I say. "Because he said this morning when I was at the Lecca sisters that this is only the beginning and it's going to get worse and worse. And that all communists should be shot, starting from the top."

Mother stops, startled, and looks at me.

"How do you know this? How do you know it's Gogu?"

"Because Gogu was at Crina and Ana's house when I went to buy bors and Ana asked him about his new Splendor roses…"

Aneta stops chewing.

"I tell you who it was…I bet it was Ana who turned him in…How do you think she gets to travel abroad to see that woman in Prague? And no one else can get a passport? I applied for a passport and never got one. Poor Geneva applied for five years for a passport and never got one, and she travels whenever she wants abroad? She has to tell them stuff about people to maintain her privileges… I bet she's an *informator*…a rat… You'd better not let Silvia go there anymore…Who knows what you say in your house and she talks about it by mistake…A child is a child, she doesn't know…Have her buy bors from someone else…"

"Well," mother says, "how do I know that someone else is not an informer as well?"

Aneta looks at mom.

"That's true. You don't know."

"Who knows what he did," mother says. "They won't take him away for just a few words. He must've done something."

"The world is upside down," says Aneta. "God help us."

She stands up.

"I'd better go now. Maybe the girls should stay inside for a while."

"Yes, it's a good idea, perhaps. Thank you for the pie, Aneta," says mom.

"Thank you, aunt Aneta," I say, my mouth full of cherries.

Aneta looks at me, caresses me gently on the top of my head and says to mom:

"They don't know what they say...A child is a child, after all..."

Before mother leaves for work that afternoon, she calls both Mirela and me in house and instructs us:

"Both of you, why don't you stay inside this afternoon, until your father comes back...stay inside and read, draw, play. Here, Mirela," she says, opening the cupboard and taking a new box of colored pencils. "Look what I've got you..."

Mirela stretches like a cat to get the pencils and opens the box, happy. She takes them out, one by one, and inspects them attentively.

"Do you like them?" I ask her after our mother leaves.

We both sit in the bed, against big pillows. I still have my "Stories from the Sea" book with me.

"Oh, yes!!!"

"Which colors do you like best?"

She ponders, then holds up the fiery red and the blue.

"These ones," she decides. "I like them both! Want to draw me something? Something beautiful?"

I consider it. Something beautiful.

"I'll draw you some fish, eh? What do you say?"

She cuddles up near me in the bed. I first have to start with the sea, I figure. The sea, the way I see it now, is an infinity of waters. Pale blue waters, surrounding me like the air, all around. And through it, many fishes, and other kinds of quick and snappy creatures, float all directions, oh, like this one, Mirela, give me the red pencil, see what beautiful spots it has on its back? See? And also his tail, oh, this one has a huge tail with big green circles, like the train of a bride dress, see? And the tail is undulating as the fish swims through the whirling waters and here, again, there is a sea turtle, and it is so slow and old and …see? It has a crooked nose.

"Like Mr. Gogu," Mirela laughs.

I take the pencil off the paper.

"See, it has exactly Mr. Gogu's nose," Mirela says again. "It's the Gogu turtle!"

I want to say something to her, but what can I say so she understands? I don't know what to think about that myself. And I don't know what to think about what Aneta said about Ana, my friend Ana, my only grown-up friend Ana, that she's an informer.

I draw fish and turtles and then many plants with long, twisted leaves, and I think about Ana. Her warm voice, and the many stories she told me. How she calls her pig "vagabond." She can not be an informer, she cannot go to police to tell them that Mr. Gogu said that all communists should be shot one by one only so she can travel to Prague, could she? My mind races from one question to another, while the paper fills with fish of all possible colors that swim in all directions in a sea so blue and bright that Mirela chirps softly, joyously, like a bird, when one more fish appears on the paper.

I return the notepad to her. Her eyes are moist with emotion.

"Like it?"

She sighs.

"Ok, time for a nap now."

She puts her pad and the pencils by the bed, on the floor. She arranges the pillow. We cuddle the best we can. Mirela is asleep in a few minutes. My eyes are wide open. I look at the ceiling and think about the sea camp. About Duck, who's at her grandma Ileana. About how all the children from our street disappeared somewhere in thin air or who knows where and won't come out. I think about the empty streets. I think about Ana telling me the story about the drunk and the tailor. The rat's daughter. Why does it have to be a rat's daughter, why couldn't it be an eagle's daughter? Or a horse's daughter? Or even a pig's daughter? Could Ana, my gentle friend who likes old tales and poetry so much, betray her own neighbor? Could she be the rat in the story? And why is it that if you are some hideous person and try to escape your fate, to better yourself, sooner or later you are back to being the disgusting thing you are?

My father's hand on my forehead wakes me up. "Wake up," he says. "What's wrong? What were you dreaming about? You were crying in your sleep."

Father is wearing something like an army uniform. It is khaki in color, with pants and a military tunic with small collar. He looks imposing in it.

"I …had… a bad dream."

Father sits on the side of the bed.

"What did you dream?"

"I can't remember," I whisper, and indeed, I don't. All I know is that I feel this immense sorrow, like something bad has just happened.

He is silent for a few seconds. He caresses my forehead.

"Dad, are you going to war?" I ask.

Mirela, who just woke up, raises her head nearby.

"Daddy, are you going to fight in a war? To shoot people? Are you going to die?" asks Mirela.

Dad caresses our heads with his big hands. First mine, then Mirela's, then mine again.

"What are you two talking about? No way I am going to die," father says.

"Daddy," resumes Mirela, "but...what if...what if... a big bear comes right now in our room, right now, in this very second, what are you going to do then?" continues Mirela, passionately.

Father smiles at her.

"If a bear comes, I'll grasp him with both my hands and smash him once so hard that he'll die instantly. Nothing will ever threaten my girls."

Mirela falls back on the pillow, satisfied.

"So you are not going to war," I say.

"There is no war," says father. "And anyway, enough worrying. Everything is going to be all right, you'll see."

"Does this mean I can still go to the camp, later on?"

Father doesn't respond.

"Can I? Later on?"

Father looks long, intensely, in my eyes, as if I am not a child - his child - but a person he tries really hard to understand.

"You'll go, Silvia," he responds. "Someday, you'll go."

He then does something he's never done before: he bends slowly and kisses me, so gently, on my forehead.

"Why don't you relax. Just relax. Dinner will be ready soon."

He then goes and starts opening pots, taking plates from the cupboard, and placing them on the table. He stirs the stew, slices bread, and pours a glass of wine for himself. I lay back on my pillow, and look up. Up there, on the white rectangle that diffuses softly toward the corners of the ceiling, is my whole life. Look. That little shadow, narrow and fragmented, stretching left to right, is our street, Milcov street, where I walk when I go to buy bors from Ana. That big blot of gray is the enemy's house, with its curtains always down, hiding the unhappiness of Mrs. Lazar over her evil son. Further on, there - do see it? - is a speck of light, and that is where Mr. Gogu lives; there, hidden in the luminous contour of a spark on my ceiling, is a garden of white roses, spellbinding in their elegance. Further to the right, do you see that little moving dot? That is where my school is; and far, far away, maybe close to the far lower corner of my room, is the seaside camp, a grain of hope hiding the mesmerizing waters of the Black Sea. In a curious way, all I know, all I know and care about, fits quite nicely in my room, in this house which I always thought was small and narrow, and now, I see, contains the world, the whole crazy world, in a few specks of dust floating around in the filtered light of the afternoon.

And then, as my father passes in front of the window to take something from a drawer, he crosses the beam of light that projects on the ceiling and everything - the world I had uncovered a few second ago, the world that revealed itself to me in minute specks of dust - is changing under my eyes, shifting geometries and redistributing accents, and now, look, a new world of shadows and dust appears, one I know nothing about.

I close my eyes. My father's kiss on my forehead brings me a peace so deep. It makes me understand, despite all my tribulations, how much I love this space around me, the confines of my narrow existence. How eager I am to understand it. Because if I understand this one, I can understand the whole wide world. And when father says that dinner is ready, I say "I'm coming, dad" but don't really move for a few moments. I give in to this quiet and comforting thought, that even when I will be a grown-up myself, even when I'll be old and wrinkled like Crina or Ana or aunt Aneta or Mr. Gogu or Duck's grandmother Ileana, I will still have to deal with this mysterious mix of lights and shadows that surrounds me right now.

"Come on, girls," father says again. "Dinner is ready. Let's eat, aren't you hungry?"

We get out of the bed, wash our hands and come to the table. Mirela grabs the crown as she passes by the night stand and puts it on her head. Father places a bowl with chicken stew in front of each of us, then brings the bread basket at the table. We each take a slice, tear small pieces of it and start eating.

I look at my father: eating in silence, lost in his thoughts, dressed in his strange military uniform. My daddy. He raises his head a bit and our eyes meet for a second. I keep looking at him but I say nothing while my mind clearly articulates: "Love you, daddy."

And my father looks closely in my eyes, smiles and, winking toward me, pours himself one more glass of wine.

76998069R00126

Made in the USA
San Bernardino, CA
18 May 2018